*'Tis the good reader that makes the good book;
in every book he finds passages which seem confidences
or asides hidden from all else and unmistakably meant
for his ear; the profit of books is according to the sensibility
of the reader; the profoundest thought or passion sleeps as
in a mine, until it is discovered by an equal mind and heart.*

RALPH WALDO EMERSON

Fräulein Else

Arthur Schnitzler

Fräulein Else

Pushkin Press
LONDON

Translated by F. H. Lyon

———

First published in Great Britain in 1925

This edition first published in 1998 by
Pushkin Press
22 Cathcart Road
London SW10 9NN

British Library Cataloguing in Publication Data:
A catalogue record for this book is available
from the British Library

British ISBN 0 901285 06 5

Printed in Spain by Litograffa Danona S. Coop
20180 Oiartzun

Jacket illustration: Duncan Ward (Private collection, London)

Illustration opposite: Georges Seurat, *The Cat*
(Private collection, New York)

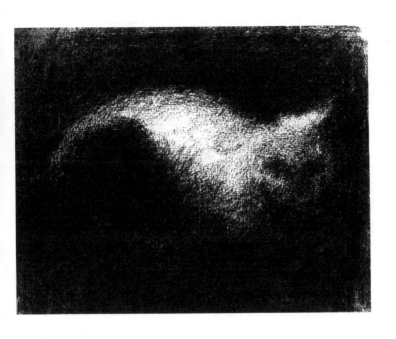

FRÄULEIN ELSE

"Won't you really play any more, Else?"

"No, Paul, I can't play any more. Good-bye. Good-bye, gnädige Frau."

"But, Else, call me Frau Cissy – or better still, just Cissy."

"Good-bye, Frau Cissy"

"But why are you going already, Else? There are two whole hours before dinner."

"Please play your single with Paul, Frau Cissy. It's really no fun playing with me today."

"Leave her alone, gnädige Frau, she's in one of her moods today ... As a matter of fact, Else, being in a bad mood is very becoming to you. And your red jersey is still more so."

"I hope you'll find me better-tempered in blue, Paul."

That was quite a good exit. I hope those two don't think I'm jealous ... I'll swear there's something between Cousin Paul and Cissy Mohr. Nothing in the world troubles me less ... Now I'll turn round again and wave to them. Wave and smile. Do I look gracious now? Oh Lord, they're playing again. I really play better than Cissy Mohr, and Paul isn't exactly a champion, but he looks nice with his open collar and that naughty boy face. If only he weren't so affected. You needn't worry, Aunt Emma ...

What a wonderful evening! It would have been the right weather today for a trip to the Rosetta Hut. How gorgeously the Cimone towers up into the sky! ... We should have started at five. Of course I should have felt miserable at first, as usual. But that wears off ... There's nothing more delightful than walking in the early morning ... That one-eyed American at the Rosetta looked like a prize-fighter. Perhaps someone knocked his eye out in a fight. I'd rather like to be married in America, but not to an American. Or I'll marry an American and we'll live in Europe. A villa on the Riviera, with marble steps going down into the sea. I'd lie on the marble with nothing on ... How long is it since we were at Menton? Seven or eight years. I was thirteen or fourteen. Ah, yes, we were better off in those days ...

It really was silly to put off the trip. We'd have been back by now at any rate ... At four o'clock, when I went out to play tennis, the express letter which Mother telegraphed to say she was sending still hadn't come. I wonder if it's come now. I could quite well have played another set ... Why do these two young men take off their hats to me? I don't know them. They've been staying at the hotel since yesterday and sit on the left-hand side of the room at meals, where the Dutch people used to sit. Did I bow ungraciously? Or even haughtily? I'm not really haughty. What was it Fred said on the way home from *Coriolanus*? High-spirited: you're high-spirited, Else, not haughty. Nice words. He always finds nice words ...

Why am I walking so slowly? Can I be afraid of Mother's letter? Well, what there is in it can hardly be pleasant. An express letter! Perhaps I've got to go home. How wretched! What a life, in spite of a red silk jersey and silk stockings – three pairs! The poor relation invited by the rich aunt. I'm sure she's sorry she asked me already. Dear Aunt, shall I put it in writing for you that I don't think of Paul even in my dreams? I don't think of anybody. I'm not in love. Not with anybody. I never have been in love. I wasn't in love even with Albert, though I imagined I was for a week. I don't think I'm capable of falling in love. That's really curious, for I'm certainly sensual. But high-spirited and ungracious too, thank Heaven! Perhaps the only time I really was in love was when I was thirteen. With Van Dyck ... and still more with the Abbé des Grieux, and with Renard, too. And when I was sixteen, at the Wörthersee ... No, that was nothing. Why am I reminiscing like this? I'm not writing my memoirs. I don't even keep a diary like Bertha. I like Fred – nothing more. Perhaps, if he had a little more style. Yes, I'm a snob. Father says I am, and laughs at me. Oh, dear father, you give me a lot of worry. I wonder if he's ever been unfaithful to Mother. I'm sure he has. Often. Mother is rather stupid. She knows nothing about me at all. No more do other people. Fred, perhaps? Well, a very little.

A heavenly evening. How splendid the hotel looks. One feels that all the people there are well-off and have no worries. I, for example. Ha, ha! It's bad luck. I was born for a care-free life. It might have been so delightful. It's bad luck ... There's a red glow over the Cimone. Paul would call it an Alpine glow. It's beautiful enough to make one cry. Oh, why have I got to go back to town?

"Good evening, Fräulein Else."

"Küss' die Hand, gnädige Frau."

"Been playing tennis?"

She can see I have, why does she ask?

"Yes, gnädige Frau. We've been playing for nearly three hours. Are you going for a walk?"

"Yes, my usual evening walk. Along the Rolleweg. It's such a pretty walk through the meadows; it's almost too sunny in the daytime."

"Yes, the meadows here are lovely. Especially from my window, by moonlight."

Good evening, Fräulein Else."

"Küss' die Hand, gnädige Frau. Good evening, Herr von Dorsday."

"Been playing tennis, Fräulein Else?"

"How observant you are, Herr von Dorsday!"

"Don't make fun of me, Else."

Why doesn't he say 'Fräulein Else'?

"Anyone who looks so charming with a racquet is justified in carrying it, to a certain extent, as an adornment."

The ass! I won't answer that at all.

"We've been playing all the afternoon. Unfortunately we were only three – Paul, Frau Mohr and I."

"I used to be a very keen tennis-player."

"And aren't you now?"

"No, I'm too old now."

"Old? Why, at Marienlyst there was a Swede who was sixty-five, and he played every evening from six till eight. And the year before he actually played in a tournament."

"Well, I'm not sixty-five yet, thank Heaven, but, unfortunately, I'm not a Swede either."

Why unfortunately? I suppose he thinks that's funny. The best thing to do is to smile politely and go.

"Küss' die Hand, gnädige Frau. Good-bye, Herr von Dorsday."

How low he bows and what eyes he makes! Calf's eyes. Perhaps I hurt his feelings by talking about the Swede of sixty-five. It doesn't matter. Frau Winawer

13

must have an unhappy life. She's certainly getting on for fifty. What tear-sacks she's got ... as if she cried a lot. Oh, how awful it must be to be so old! Herr von Dorsday pays a lot of attention to her. There he is walking beside her. He's still quite nice-looking with his pointed beard, going grey. But I don't like him. He's a social climber. What good does your first-class tailor do you, Herr von Dorsday? Dorsday! I'm sure your name used to be something else ... Here comes that sweet little girl of Cissy's with her Fräulein.

"Hello, Fritzi. Bon soir, Mademoiselle. Vous allez bien?"
"Merci, Mademoiselle. Et vous?"
"Why, Fritzi, you've got an alpenstock. Are you going up the Cimone?"
"On, no, I'm not allowed to go as high as that yet."
"You'll be allowed to next year all right. So long, Fritzi. A bientôt, Mademoiselle."
"Bon soir, Mademoiselle."

A pretty girl. I wonder why she's a nurse – and Cissy's into the bargain. A hard fate. Oh well I may come to that too. No, I'll certainly find something better to do. Better? ... What a lovely evening! 'The air is like champagne,' Dr. Waldberg said yesterday. And the day before yesterday someone else said it ...

14

Why do people sit in the lounge in this wonderful weather? I can't understand it. Or are they all waiting for express letters? The porter has seen me. If there'd been an express letter for me he'd have brought it to me at once. So there isn't one. Thank Heaven! I'll lie down for a bit before dinner. 'Dinner' – why does Cissy use the English word? Silly affectation. They're a good match, Cissy and Paul ... Oh, I wish the letter was here. It'll probably come during dinner. And if it doesn't come I shall have a bad night. I slept so wretchedly last night, too. I'll take some veronal tonight ... No, my dear Fred, you mustn't worry about me. One ought to try everything, even hashish. That young naval officer, Brandel, has brought some with him – from China, I think. Does one drink hashish or smoke it? It's supposed to give one marvellous visions. Brandel invited me to drink – or smoke – hashish with him. A cheeky boy. But nice-looking.

"A letter for you, Fräulein."
The porter! Now for it. I turn round quite casually. It might be a letter from Caroline, or from Bertha, or from Fred, or Miss Jackson ...
"Thank you."
Yes, it is from Mother – an express letter. Why didn't he say it was an express letter?

15

"Oh, an express letter!"

I shan't open it till I get to my room and then I'll read it all by myself ... The Marchesa. How young she looks in the half-light. I'm sure she's forty-five. Where shall I be at forty-five? Dead, perhaps. I hope so. She smiles at me as pleasantly as she always does. I'll let her pass with a slight nod; I mustn't let her think I feel specially honoured by being smiled at by a Marchesa ...

"Buona sera."

She says buona sera to me. Now I must bow at any rate. Was my bow too deep? She is so much older. How splendidly she carries herself. I wonder if she's divorced. I carry myself well, too, but – I know. That's what makes the difference ...

An Italian might be dangerous to me. It's a pity the dark man with the Roman head left so soon. Paul said he looked a rascal. Suppose he is? I've nothing against rascals. Quite the opposite ... Well, here I am at number 77. A lucky number. It's a pretty room. Pinewood furniture. There stands my virginal bed ... now it's a real Alpine glow. But I shan't admit it to Paul. You know, Paul's shy. A doctor – a woman's doctor! Perhaps that's just why. The day before yesterday in the woods, when we were so far ahead, he might have been a bit more enterprising. Not that it would have done him any good. No one has ever been really enterprising with me. Except perhaps at the Wörthersee three years ago, when we were bathing. Enterprising? No, he was simply objectionable. But how handsome. An Apollo Belvedere. I really didn't understand anything then. After all, I was only sixteen ... My heavenly meadow! Mine! I wish I could take it back to Vienna. A light mist. Autumn? Well, it's the 3rd of September, and we're high up in the mountains.

Well now, Fräulein Else, can't you make up your mind to read that letter? It needn't have anything to do with Father. Mightn't it be something about my brother? Perhaps he's got engaged to one of his flames. A chorus girl or a girl in a glove shop. Oh no, he's got too much sense for that. As a matter of fact, I don't know much about him. When I was sixteen and he was twenty-one we were really good friends for a time. He told me a great deal about someone called Lotte; then all of a sudden he stopped. Lotte must have done something to him. And since then he's never told me anything more ... Why, the letter's open, and I never noticed that I was opening it. I'll sit down on the window-sill and read it. I must take care I don't fall out ... According to a telegram from San Martino, an unfortunate accident has occurred at the Hotel Fratazza. Fräulein Else T., a beautiful girl of nineteen, daughter of the well-known lawyer ... Of course they'd say I'd killed myself because I was crossed in love, or because I was expecting ... Crossed in love – no.

"My dear child" ... I'll look at the end first ... *"So once more, don't be angry with us, my darling child, and be a thousand times – "* good Heavens, they haven't killed themselves! No, if they had I'd have had a telegram from Rudi ... *"My dear child, you can understand how sorry I am to burst into your pleasant holiday time"* – as if it wasn't always holiday time for me, worse luck –" *with such unpleasant news"* ... Mother does write a fearful style ... *"But after mature consideration I have really no other choice. To cut it short, Father's situation has become acute. I don't know what to think or do"* ... Why all this talk? ... *"The sum in question is a comparatively trivial one, thirty thousand gulden"* – trivial? – *"which must be forthcoming in three days, or all is lost"* ... Heavens, what does she mean? *"Imagine, my dear, Baron Höning"* – what, the Public Prosecutor"? – *"sent for Father this morning. You know how highly the Baron thinks of Father, how fond he is of him, indeed. A year and a half ago, when things hung by a thread, he spoke to the principal creditors in person and put things straight at the last moment. But this time absolutely nothing can be done if the money is not forthcoming. And quite apart from our all being ruined, there will be such a scandal as there never was before. Think of it – a*

lawyer, a famous lawyer, who – no, I cannot write it down. I am fighting with my tears all the time I write. *You know, my dear, for you are intelligent, we have been in a situation like this several times before, and the family has always helped us out. Last time it was a question of 120,000 gulden. But then Father had to sign an undertaking never to approach our relations again, especially Uncle Bernhard"* ... Well, go on, go on, what's she driving at? What can I do about it? ..."*The only one of whom I can think as a last resort is Uncle Victor, but unfortunately he is on a trip to the North Cape or Scotland"* – yes, he's well off, the horrid creature – *"and is absolutely unreachable, at least for the time being. Father's colleagues are out of the question, especially Dr. Sch., who has often helped Father out before,"* – good Heavens, how do we stand with him? – *"now that he has married again"* ... Well, what what, WHAT do you want me to do? ... *"And now your letter has come, my dear child, in which you mention among other people Dorsday, who is also staying at the Fratazza, and it seemed to us like the hand of providence. You know how often Dorsday used to come to our house in years gone by"* ... Yes, very often ... *"It is the merest chance that we have seen less of him in the last two or three years; he is supposed to be deeply entangled – nothing very grand between ourselves"* ... Why 'between ourselves'? ... *"Father still plays whist with him every Thursday at the Residenzklub, and last winter he saved him a big sum of money in an action against another art-dealer.*

19

Besides, why shouldn't you know it, he helped Father once before" ... I thought as much ... *"It was only a very small sum that time – eight thousand gulden – but, after all, thirty is nothing to Dorsday. So I wondered whether you could not do us a kindness and speak to Dorsday"* ... What? ... *"He has always been particularly fond of you"* ... I haven't noticed it. He stroked my cheek once, when I was twelve or thirteen, and said 'Quite a grown-up young lady already' ... *"And as Father, luckily, has not approached him again since the eight thousand, he will probably not refuse to do him this favour. He is supposed to have made eighty thousand quite lately on a Rubens which he sold to America. Of course you mustn't mention this"* – do you take me for a fool, Mother? – *"but otherwise you can talk to him quite frankly. You might also mention, if occasion arises, that Baron Höning has sent for Father, and that if we get thirty thousand the worst will be averted, not only for the time being, but, God willing, for ever,"* – do you really think so, Mother? – *"for the Erbesheimer case, which is going on splendidly, will certainly bring Father in a hundred thousand, but of course he cannot ask the Erbesheimers for anything at the present stage of the case. So I beg you, my dear child, to speak to Dorsday. I assure you there is no harm in it. Father could simply have telegraphed to him – we seriously considered doing so – but it is quite a different matter, dear, when one talks to a person face to face. The money must be here on the 5th, at noon. Dr. F."* – who is Dr. F.? oh yes,

Fiala – *"is inexorable. Of course personal rancour enters into the matter, but as, unfortunately, trust money is concerned"* – good God, Father, what have you done? – *"there is nothing to be done. And if the money is not in Fiala's hands by twelve noon on the 5th, a warrant will be issued; Baron Höning will keep it back till then. So Dorsday would have to telegraph the sum to Dr. F. through his bank. Then we shall be saved. Otherwise God knows what will happen. Believe me, you will not be lowering yourself in the least, my darling child. Father had scruples at first. He even made efforts in two further directions. But he came home quite desperate"* – can Father ever be desperate? – *"not so much, perhaps, because of the money as because people behave so shamefully to him. One of them was once Father's best friend. You can guess whom I mean"* ... I can't guess at all. Father has had so many best friends, and in reality not one. Warnsdorf, perhaps? ... *"Father came home at one o'clock and now it is four in the morning. He is asleep at last, thank God"* ... It would be the best thing for him if he never woke up ... *"I shall post this letter myself as early as possible, express, so that you will get it on the morning of the 3rd"* ... What made Mother think that? She never knows anything about such things. *"So speak to Dorsday at once, I beseech you, and telegraph at once how it goes. Don't let Aunt Emma notice anything, for Heaven's sake. It is sad that in a case like this one cannot turn to one's own sister, but one might just as well speak to a stone. My dear, dear child, I am so sorry that you should have to go through such things in your youth, but believe me, Father himself is the last to blame"* ... Who is then, Mother? ... *"Let us hope that the Erbesheimer case will mean the turning of a new leaf in our existence in every respect. We have only to get through these few weeks. It would surely be an irony of Fate if a catastrophe happened over the thirty thousand gulden...."* She doesn't seriously mean that Father would commit ... but wouldn't ... the other thing be even worse? ... *"Now I must stop, dear. I hope that in any case"* – in any case? – *"you will be able to stay at San Martino until the 9th or 10th at least. You must certainly not return on our account. Give my love to your Aunt; go on being nice to her. So once more, don't be angry with us my darling child, and be a thousand times – "* ... Yes, I know that bit.

So I am to borrow from Herr von Dorsday ... Madness! How can Mother imagine such a thing? Why didn't Father simply get into the train and come straight here? He'd have come just as quick as the express letter. But perhaps they'd have suspected him of trying to get away and arrested him at the station ... It's awful, simply awful! And even if we get the thirty thousand we shan't be out of the wood. It's always been the same story for the last seven years – no, longer than that. Who'd think it to look at me? No one would think it to look at me, or Father either. And yet everybody knows it. It's a mystery how we can still hold our heads up. One gets used to everything. And in spite of it we live quite well. Mother's really an artist. The dinner for fourteen people last New Year's Day – incomprehensible. But my two pairs of evening gloves – there was a regular fuss about them. And when Rudi wanted three hundred gulden the other day, Mother almost cried. And Father is always in good spirits. Always? No. Oh no. At the opera the other day – at *Figaro* – his eyes suddenly lost all expression; I was terrified. He seemed to become quite another person. But we had supper afterwards at the Grand Hotel, and then he was in as splendid spirits as ever.

Here I am with the letter in my hand. The letter's crazy. I speak to Dorsday? I'd die of shame ... Why should I be ashamed? It's not my fault ... How if I were to speak to Aunt Emma? Nonsense. She probably hasn't got so much money. Uncle is a miser. Oh God, why haven't I any money? Why haven't I earned anything yet? Why haven't I learnt anything? Oh, I have learnt something! Who can say I haven't learnt anything? I can play the piano; I know French, English and a little Italian; I've been to lectures on the history of art. Ha, ha! And if I had learnt anything more practical, what good would it be to me now? I certainly couldn't have saved thirty thousand gulden already.

The Alpine glow has died out. The evening isn't wonderful any longer. The landscape is gloomy. No, it isn't the landscape, but life itself that's gloomy. And I'm sitting quietly on the window-sill, and Father is to be locked up. No! Never, never! It musn't be! I'll save him! Yes, Father, I'll save you! It's quite simple. A few nonchalant words; it's just in my line – 'high-spirited.' Ha, ha! I'll treat Herr von Dorsday as if it were an honour for him to lend us money. So it is an honour for him to lend us money. So it is an honour ... 'Herr von Dorsday, might I trouble you for a moment? I've just had a letter from Mother. She is in a temporary embarrassment – or rather Father is.' 'Why, of course, my dear young lady, with the greatest pleasure. What is the sum in question?' ... If only I didn't dislike him so much – and the way he looks at me. No, Herr Dorsday, I'm not taken in by your smartness and your monocle and your title. You might just as well deal in old clothes as in old pictures ... But, Else, Else, what are you thinking of? Oh, I can permit myself a remark like that. Nobody notices it in me. I'm positively blonde, a reddish blonde, and Rudi looks a regular aristocrat. Certainly one can notice it at once in Mother, at any rate in her speech, but not at all in Father. For that matter, let people notice it. I don't deny it, and I'm sure Rudi doesn't. Quite the

24

contrary. What would Rudi do if Father were put in prison? Would he shoot himself? Nonsense! Shootings and criminal cases, all those things don't happen, they're only in the papers.

The air is like champagne. In an hour it'll be time for dinner. I can't bear Cissy. She doesn't care a scrap about her little girl. What shall I wear? The blue or the black? Perhaps the black would be more correct today. Too décolleté? *Toilette de circonstance*, as they say in French novels. At all events I must look bewitching when I talk to Dorsday. After dinner, quite casually. His eyes will be fixed on my décolletage. Odious creature. I hate him. I hate everybody. Must it be Dorsday? Is Dorsday really the only person in the world who has thirty thousand gulden? Suppose I speak to Paul. If he told Aunt Emma that he had gambling debts he'd certainly be able to get the money.

It's nearly dark now. Night. The dead of night. I wish I was dead ... It simply isn't true. Couldn't I go down now, at once, and speak to Dorsday before dinner? Oh, how horrible! ... Paul, if you get me thirty thousand you can have anything you ask of me. That's out of a novel. The noble daughter sells herself for her beloved father's sake, and really rather enjoys it. B-r-r! No, Paul, you can't get me even for thirty thousand. Nobody can. But for a

25

million? ... Or for a palace? For a pearl necklace?
If I marry some day I shall probably do it cheaper.
Is it really so bad? Fanny sold herself. She told me
herself that her husband makes her shudder. How
would you like it, Father, if I sold myself by auction
this evening? To save you from prison? It would
make a sensation! I'm feverish, I'm sure. Perhaps it's
the air. Like champagne ... If Fred were here,
could he give me advice? I don't need any advice.
There's no advice to give. I'll talk to Herr von
Dorsday d'Eperies and I'll borrow from him – I, the
high-spirited one, the aristocrat, the Marchesa, the
beggar girl, the swindler's daughter! How have I
come to this? How have I come to this? No other
woman climbs as well as I do, no other has so much
go. I'm a sporting girl. I ought to have been born in
England, or a Countess.

There are my clothes hanging in the wardrobe.
Has the green been paid for, Mother? Only one
instalment, I think. I'll wear the black. They all
stared at me yesterday, even the pale little man with
the gold pince-nez. I'm not really pretty, but I'm
interesting. I ought to have gone on the stage. Bertha
has had three lovers already, and no one thinks the
worse of her for it. At Düsseldorf it was the manager.
At Hamburg she lived with a married man at the
Atlantic Hotel – a suite with a bathroom. I believe

she's proud of it. They're all stupid. I'll have a hundred lovers, a thousand; why not? The décolletage isn't low enough; if I was married it could be lower ... 'How lucky that I should have met you, Herr von Dorsday; I've just had a letter from Vienna' ... I'll take the letter with me in case of emergencies. Shall I ring for the chambermaid? No, I'll dress alone. I don't need any help with the black dress. If I was rich I'd never travel without a maid.

I must turn on the light. It's getting chilly. Shut the window. Blind down? No need. There's no one standing on the mountain over there with a telescope. Worse luck ... 'I've just had a letter, Herr von Dorsday' ... Perhaps it'll be better to do it after dinner. One is in a lighter mood then. Dorsday will be too ... I might drink a glass of wine first. But I should certainly enjoy my dinner more if I finished the whole business first. Pudding *à la merveille, fromage et fruits divers*. But what if Herr von Dorsday should say no? Or if he's downright impudent? Oh no; no one has ever been impudent to me. Well, Lieutenant Brandel was, but he didn't mean any harm. I've got a bit thinner again. It suits me ... The twilight stares in. It stares in like a ghost – like a hundred ghosts. Ghost are rising up out of my meadow. How far off is Vienna? How long have I been away? How alone I am! I haven't a girl friend, nor a man friend.

Where are they all? Whom shall I marry? Who would marry a swindler's daughter? ... 'I've just had a letter, Herr von Dorsday' ... 'Oh, Fräulein Else, it's not worth mentioning, I sold a Rembrandt only yesterday, you put me to shame, Fräulein Else' ... And now he's tearing a page out of his cheque book and signing it with his gold fountain pen; and tomorrow morning I'll go to Vienna with the cheque. I'll do that anyhow, cheque or no cheque. I won't stay here any longer. I simply couldn't. I live here as a smart young lady while Father has one foot in the grave – or rather in the dock? ...

The last pair of silk stockings but one. Nobody'll notice the little tear just below the knee. No one? Who knows? Don't be flippant, Else ... Bertha's a hussy. But is Christine a scrap better? Her future husband can congratulate himself. I'm sure Mother has always been a faithful wife. But I shan't be faithful. I'm high-spirited, but I shan't be faithful. Rascals are too dangerous for me. I'm sure the Marchesa has a rogue for her lover. If Fred really knew me there'd be an end to his respect for me. 'You could have been anything, Fräulein, a pianist, or a bookkeeper, or an actress; there are so many possibilities in you. But you have always been too well off.' Too well off! Ha, ha! Fred over-estimates me. I've really no talent for anything ... Who knows! I might have

gone as far as Bertha by this time. But I lack energy.
Young lady of good family. Ha, ha, good family!
The father misappropriates trust money. Why are
you doing this to me, Father? If only you had something to show for it! But to gamble it away on the
Bourse – was it worth the trouble? And the thirty
thousand won't help you either. For three months
perhaps. But in the end he'll have to clear out. It
had nearly come to that eighteen months ago. Then
help came. But some day help won't come. And
what will happen to us then? Rudi'll go to the
Vanderhulsts' bank at Rotterdam. And I? A good
match. Oh, if I laid myself out for that! I'm really
pretty today. It's probably the excitement. For
whom am I pretty? Should I be happier if Fred was
here? Oh, Fred's nothing to me. He isn't a rascal.
But I'd take him if he'd got money. And then a rascal would come along – and it'd be all up ... You'd
like to be a rascal, wouldn't you, Herr von Dorsday?
At a distance you sometimes look like one. Like a
dissipated Vicomte, like a Don Juan – with your stupid monocle and your white flannel suit. But you're
not a rascal by a long way ...

Have I got everything? Am I ready for dinner? ...
But what shall I do for a whole hour if I don't meet
Dorsday? If he's out walking with the unhappy Frau
Winawer? She isn't unhappy at all, she doesn't need

thirty thousand gulden. Well, then, I'll sit down in the lounge, look magnificent in an armchair, skim the *Illustrated News* and the *Vie Parisienne*, cross my legs – no one will notice the tear below the knee. Perhaps a millionaire has just arrived ... You or no one ... I'll take the white shawl, it suits me. I'll throw it carelessly round my beautiful shoulders. For whom have I beautiful shoulders? I could make a man very happy – if the right man only came along. But children I won't have. I'm not motherly. Marie Weil is motherly. Mother is motherly. Aunt Irene is motherly. I have a noble brow and a beautiful figure ... 'If only I might paint you as I should like to, Fräulein Else' ... Yes, I've no doubt that would suit you. I don't even remember his name. It certainly wasn't Titian; so it was an impertinence ... 'I've just got a letter, Herr von Dorsday' ... A little more powder on my neck and throat, a drop of verveine on my handkerchief, shut the wardrobe, open the window again – oh, how marvellous! To weeping point! I'm nervous. Isn't one entitled to be nervous in circumstances like these? The box with the veronal in it is among my chemises. I ought to have new chemises too. There'll be another fuss about that. Oh Lord!

The Cimone looks uncanny, gigantic, as if it were ready to fall on me. Not a star in the sky as yet. The

air is like champagne. And the perfume from the
meadows! I'll live in the country. I'll marry a
landowner and have children. Dr. Froriep, perhaps,
was the only man I should have been happy with.
How delightful those two evenings were – the first at
Kniep's and the second at the Artists' Ball. Why did
he disappear so suddenly – for me at any rate?
Because of Father, perhaps? Probably. I should like to
send out a greeting into the air before I go downstairs
again among the rabble. But to whom shall I send my
greeting? I'm all alone. No one can imagine how terribly alone I am. Hail, my lover! Who? Hail, my
bridegroom! Who? Hail, my friend! Who?
Fred? ... Not he. I'll leave the windows open, even if
it is turning chilly. Turn the light off. There ... Yes,
of course, the letter. I must take it with me for all
eventualities. The book on the table by the bed; I simply must read a bit more of *Notre Cœur* tonight, whatever happens. Good evening, lovely girl in the look-
ing-glass, have pleasant memories of me, goodbye! ...

Why do I lock the door? There's no stealing here.
Does Cissy leave her door open at night, or does she
only open it to him when he knocks? Is it quite certain? Of course it is. Then they lie in bed together.
Disgusting! I won't share a bedroom with my husband and my thousand lovers ...

31

No one at all on the stairs! There never is anyone at this time. My steps echo. I've been here three weeks now. I left Gmunden on the 12th of August. Gmunden was dull. Where did Father get the money to send Mother and me to the country? And Rudi was away for four whole weeks. God knows where. He didn't write twice during the whole time. I shall never understand our existence. Certainly Mother has no jewellery left ... Why was Fred only two days at Gmunden? He's got a mistress too, for certain – though I can't imagine it. I can't imagine anything. He hasn't written to me for a whole week. He writes nice letters ... Who's that sitting at the little table? No, it isn't Dorsday. Thank God for that. It would be impossible to say anything to him now before dinner ... Why is the porter looking at me so oddly? Did he read Mother's express letter? I think I'm crazy. I must give him another tip soon ... The fair woman over there is dressed for dinner already. How can anybody be so fat? ... I'll go out in front of the hotel and walk up and down a bit. Or shall I go to the music-room? Isn't someone playing in there? A Beethoven sonata! How can anyone play a Beethoven sonata in this place? I'm neglecting my piano-playing. I shall practise regularly again in Vienna. In fact, I'll start an entirely new life. We must all do that. Things can't go on like this. I shall talk to Father seriously – if it isn't too late. It won't be too late, it won't. Why have I never done it before? Everything at home is settled with jokes, and no one feels like joking. Everyone is afraid of the other, and everyone is alone. Mother is alone, because she isn't clever enough and doesn't know anything about anyone – about me, or Rudi, or Father. But she doesn't realise it, no more does Rudi. He's a nice fellow, good-looking and well turned out, but he promised more when he was twenty-one. It'll do him good to go to Holland. But where shall I go? I'd like to travel and be able to do as I pleased. If Father bolts to America I'll go with him ... I feel quite confused ... The porter will think me mad – sitting on this sofa staring into space. I'll light a cigarette. Where's my cigarette case? Upstairs. But where? I put the veronal in with my linen, but where did I put the cigarette case? ...

Here come Cissy and Paul. She had to dress for dinner some time, or they'd have gone on playing in the dark ... They don't see me. I wonder what he's saying to her. Why does she laugh so inanely? It would be fun to write an anonymous letter to her husband in Vienna. Could I do such a thing? Never. Who knows? Now they've seen me. I'll nod to them. She's annoyed because I look so pretty. How embarassed she is.

"Dressed for dinner already, Else?"

"As you see, Frau Cissy."

"You really look charming, Else. I should so like to make love to you."

"Save yourself the trouble, Paul, and give me a cigarette instead."

"With the greatest pleasure."

"Thank you. How did the singles go?"

"Frau Cissy beat me three times running."

"He was absent-minded. By the way Else, do you know that the Crown Prince of Greece is coming tomorrow?"

What do I care about the Crown Prince of Greece?

"Oh, really?"

Heavens! there's Dorsday with Frau Winawer. They're bowing to me. Now they're going on. I returned the bow too politely. Quite differently from my usual way. Oh, what a creature I am!

"Your cigarette's out, Else."

"Give me another match, then, please. Thank you."

"Your shawl is very pretty, Else; with the black dress it suits you wonderfully. And now I must go and dress too."

I wish she wouldn't go away, I'm afraid of Dorsday.

"And I've ordered the hairdresser for seven o'clock. She's splendid. She's at Milan in the winter. Well, good-bye, Else, good-bye, Paul."

"Küss' die Hand, gnädige Frau."

"Good-bye, Frau Cissy."

She's gone. I'm glad Paul's staying, at least.

"May I sit with you for a moment, Else, or am I disturbing you in your dreams?"

"Why in my dreams? Perhaps in my realities?"

That means nothing whatever. I'd rather he went. I've got to speak to Dorsday. There he is, still standing with the unhappy Frau Winawer. He's bored, I can see it; he'd like to come over to me.

"Then there are realities in which you prefer not to be disturbed?"

What's he saying? He can go to the devil. Why am I smiling at him so coquettishly? I don't mean it for him at all. Dorsday's leering across. Where am I?

"What's the matter with you today, Else?"

"What should be the matter?"

"You're mysterious, demonic, seductive."

"Don't talk nonsense, Paul."

"It's enough to send one mad to look at you!"

What is he thinking of? What is he saying to me? He's good-looking. My cigarette smoke clings to his hair. But I've no use for him now.

"You look past me all the time. Why do you do it, Else?"

I won't answer at all. I've no use for him now. I'll put on my most insupportable expression. Only no conversation.

"Your thoughts are somewhere else."

"That's quite possible."

He's nothing to me. Does Dorsday notice that I'm
waiting for him? I'm not looking his way, but I know
he's looking at me.

"Well then, good-bye, Else."

Thank God! He's kissing my hand. He never does
that as a rule.

"Good-bye, Paul."

Where did I get that melting voice from? He's
going, the humbug! Probably he has to arrange
something with Cissy about tonight. I wish him joy.
I'll put my shawl round my shoulders and get up
and go out in front of the hotel. Certainly it'll be
rather chilly. A pity that my coat – ah, I hung it up
in the porter's office this morning. I can feel
Dorsday's look on the back of my neck, through the
shawl. Frau Winawer is going up to her room now.
How do I know? Telepathy.

"Excuse me, porter –"

"Do you want your coat, Fräulein?"

"Yes, please."

*"The evenings are a bit chilly already, Fräulein. It comes
on so suddenly here."*

"Thank you."

Shall I really go out in front of the hotel? Of
course, why not?" At least to the door. Here they
come, one after the other. The man with the gold
pince-nez, the tall fair man with the green waistcoat;

they all look at me. The little Geneva girl is pretty.
No, she's from Lausanne. It really isn't so cold.

"Good evening, Fräulein Else."

Good Heavens, it's him. I won't say anything
about Father. Not a word. Not till after dinner. Or
I'll go to Vienna tomorrow. I'll go to Dr. Fiala
myself. Why didn't I think of that at once? I turn
around as if I didn't know who was behind me.

"Oh, Herr von Dorsday."

"Are you going for a walk, Fräulein Else?"

*"Well, not exactly a walk, just a stroll up and down before
dinner."*

"We have nearly an hour."

"Really?"

It really isn't so cold. The mountains are blue. It
would be jolly if he suddenly proposed to me.

"There isn't a lovelier spot in the world than this."

*"Do you think so, Herr von Dorsday? But please don't tell
me that the air is like champagne."*

*"No, Fräulein Else, I only say that from six thousand feet
up. And here we are hardly five thousand feet above sea level."*

"Does that make so much difference?"

"Of course. Were you ever in the Engadine?"

"No, never. Is the air there really like champagne?"

*"One could almost say that. But champagne is not my
favourite drink. I prefer this part, if only for the wonderful
woods."*

37

How boring he is! Doesn't he see it himself? He obviously doesn't know what to talk about to me. It would be simpler with a married woman. One just says something a bit risqué, and the conversation is well under way.

"Are you staying some time at San Martino, Fräulein Else?"

Idiotic. Why do I look at him so coquettishly? He's smiling already, in the usual way. Oh, how stupid men are!

"That depends partly on my Aunt's plans."

That's quite untrue. As if I couldn't go to Vienna alone.

"Probably till the 10th."

"I suppose your mother is still at Gmunden."

"No, Herr von Dorsday, she's been back in Vienna for three weeks. Father is in Vienna too. He's hardly taken a week's holiday this year. I think the Erbesheimer case is giving him a lot of work."

"I can imagine that. But your father is probably the only man who can get Erbesheimer out of his scrape. The fact that the case has become a civil action is in itself a success."

That's good, that's good.

"I'm glad to hear you have so favourable a premonition."

"Premonition? What do you mean"

"Why, that Father will win the case for Erbesheimer."

"I would not go so far as definitely to say that."

What, is he retreating? I won't allow that.

"Oh, I have some belief in premonitions and feelings. Think, Herr von Dorsday, I got a letter from home only today."

That wasn't very clever. He looks rather puzzled. But go on, don't stumble. He's a good old friend of Father's. Go on. Go on. Now, or never!

"Herr von Dorsday, you spoke so kindly about Father just now that it would be simply horrid of me not to be quite straight-forward with you."

What calf's eyes he is making at me! Oh dear, he notices something. Go on, go on.

"You were mentioned in that letter, Herr von Dorsday. It was a letter from Mother."

"Really?"

"It was a very sad letter. You know how things are in our family, Herr von Dorsday" ...

Good Heavens, my voice is breaking. Forward, forward, there's no retreat now – thank God!

"To cut it short, Herr von Dorsday, things have come to a crisis again" ... Now he'd like to disappear ... *"The sum in question – is a trifle. Really only a trifle, Herr von Dorsday. And yet, Mother writes, everything depends on it."*

I'm stumbling on as stupidly as a cow.

"Please calm yourself, Fräulein Else."

He said that nicely. But he needn't touch my arm all the same.

"What is the matter, Fräulein Else? What was in the sad letter from your mother?"

"Herr von Dorsday, Father" ... my knees are trembling ... *"Mother writes that Father – "*

"For goodness' sake, Else, what is the matter? Wouldn't you rather – here's a seat. Won't you put your coat on? It's rather chilly."

"Thanks, Herr von Dorsday. Oh, it's nothing – nothing particular."

Here I am all of a sudden sitting on the bench. Who's the lady coming this way? I don't know her at all. If only I hadn't got to go on talking! How he looks at me! How could you ask this of me, Father? It wasn't right of you, Father. But now it's happened. I ought to have waited till after dinner ...

"Well, Fräulein Else?"

His monocle's dangling. It looks silly. Shall I answer him? I must. Quickly, then, and get it over. After all, what can happen to me? He's an old friend of Father's.

"Well, Herr von Dorsday, you're an old friend of our family." I said that very well. *"And you probably won't be surprised when I tell you that Father is in a terrible mess again."*

How strange my voice sounds! Is it me speaking? Am I dreaming? I'm sure I must look quite different, too, from what I usually do.

"It certainly does not surprise me very much. You're right there, Fräulein Else ... although at the same time I regret it deeply."

40

Why do I look up to him so beseechingly? Smile, smile! It's going all right.

"I have a sincere feeling of friendship for your father – for all of you."

He oughtn't to look at me like that, it's not decent. I'll speak differently and not smile. I must behave with more dignity.

"Well, Herr von Dorsday, now you will have an opportunity of proving your friendship for my father." Thank Heaven, I have got my old voice back. *"It seems, Herr von Dorsday, that all our friends and relations ... most of them are not back in Vienna yet ... otherwise Mother would probably not have thought of it. The other day, in a letter to Mother, I casually mentioned your being at San Martino – among other things, of course."*

"I didn't suppose, Fräulein Else, that I was the sole subject of your correspondence with your mother."

Why does he press his knee against mine? And I allow it. But what does it matter? When once one has sunk so low ...

"This is how things stand. It's Dr. Fiala who seems to be making particular difficulties for Father this time."

"Oh, Dr. Fiala."

He evidently knows what kind of person this Fiala is ...

"Yes, Dr. Fiala. And the sum which is owing must be sent on the 5th – that is the day after tomorrow – at twelve noon,

41

... or rather it must be in his hands by then, otherwise Baron Höning ... yes, just think, the Baron sent for Father privately, he's very fond of him."

What am I talking about Höning for? There was no need to.

"You mean, Else, that otherwise an arrest would be inevitable?"

Why does he say it so disagreeably? I won't answer, I'll just nod ... "Yes." Now I've said yes after all.

"H'm, that's – er – bad, that's really very – er – such a very gifted, brilliant man ... And what is the sum in question, Fräulein Else?"

Why does he smile? He says it's bad, and he smiles. What does his smile mean? That the amount is of no consequence to him? And if he says no? I'll kill myself if he says no! So I'm to name the sum.

"What, Herr von Dorsday, didn't I tell you how much it is? A million."

Why did I say that? It's not time for joking. But when I tell him how much less it is really, he'll be pleased. How he opens his eyes! Does he really think it possible that Father could ask him for a million?

"Forgive me, Herr von Dorsday, for joking at such a time. I can assure you I don't feel like joking."

Yes, yes, press your knee against mine, you may do it ...

"Of course the sum isn't a million. The total amount is

thirty thousand gulden, Herr von Dorsday, which must be in Dr. Fiala's hands by noon the day after tomorrow. Yes. Mother writes that Father has made every possible effort, but, as I said, the relations who could have helped us are not in Vienna" ... Oh God, how I am humiliating myself! ... *"Otherwise, Father would certainly not have thought of turning to you, Herr von Dorsday, or of asking me —"*

Why doesn't he speak? Why doesn't he move a muscle? Why doesn't he say yes? Where's the cheque-book and the fountain pen? Heavens, he isn't going to say no? Shall I throw myself on my knees before him? Oh God! Oh God! ...

"On the 5th, you said, Fräulein Else?"

Thank God, he's speaking ... *"Yes, the day after tomorrow, Herr von Dorsday, at twelve noon. So that it'll be necessary to — I don't think it could be done by letter now"* ...

"Of course not, Fräulein Else, we should have to telegraph."

'We' — that's good, very good.

"That would be the smallest part of the business. How much did you say, Else?"

He heard, why does he torture me?

"Thirty thousand, Herr von Dorsday. Really an absurdly small sum."

Why did I say that? How silly! But he's smiling. What a silly girl, he's thinking. He's smiling quite amiably. Father's saved. He'd have lent him fifty

43

thousand while he was about it, and we could have got ourselves all kinds of things. I'd have bought myself some new chemises. How mean I am! One becomes like that ...

"Not so absurdly small, my dear child" – Why does he say 'my dear child'? is it a good sign or not? – *"as you imagine. Even thirty thousand gulden take some earning."*

"I beg your pardon, Herr von Dorsday. I didn't mean that. I only thought how sad it was that Father – because of such a sum, such a trifle" – Oh Lord, I'm getting muddled again! *"You can't imagine, Herr von Dorsday, even if you do know something about our circumstances, how terrible it is for me, and more especially for Mother."*

He's putting one foot on the seat. Is that supposed to be good form, or what?

"Oh, I can easily imagine it, dear Else" ...

What a strange tone there is in his voice, quite different from what it was.

"And I've often thought myself, how sad it is about this brilliant man."

Why does he say it's 'sad'? Won't he hand over the money? No, he only means it in a general sense. Why doesn't he say yes once and for all? Or does he take that for granted? How he looks at me! Why doesn't he go on speaking? Oh, because the two Hungarian ladies are passing. At any rate he's standing properly now, not with one foot on the seat. His tie is too loud for an elderly man. Does his mistress choose them for him? Nothing very grand 'between ourselves,' Mother writes. Thirty thousand gulden! But I'm smiling at him. Why am I smiling. Oh, I'm a coward!

"If only one could take it for granted that this sum would do any good! But you're a sensible girl, Else — what would thirty thousand gulden be? A drop in the bucket."

Oh Heavens, won't he give me the money? I musn't look so frightened. Everything is at stake. I must say something intelligent and convincing.

"Oh no, Herr von Dorsday, this time it wouldn't be a drop in the bucket. The Erbesheimer case is coming on, don't forget that, Herr von Dorsday, and it's as good as won already. And Father has other cases, too. Besides, I mean — you mustn't laugh, Herr von Dorsday — to talk very seriously to Father. He pays some attention to me. I may say that if anyone can influence him at all it is me."

"You are certainly a delightful, charming creature, Fräulein Else."

There's that tone in his voice again. I hate it when that tone comes into men's voices. I don't like it even in Fred.

"A charming creature indeed."

Why does he say 'indeed'? It's banal. They only say that at the Burgtheater.

"But much as I should like to share your optimism — when once the car has gone off the rails — "

"Not this time, Herr von Dorsday. If I didn't completely believe in Father, if I weren't completely convinced that these thirty thousand gulden —"

I don't know what more to say. I can't absolutely beg him. He's thinking it over. Obviously. Perhaps he doesn't know Fiala's address. Nonsense. The situation's impossible. I sit here like a poor sinner. He stands in front of me and stares at me through his monocle and says nothing. I'll get up now, that'll be best. I won't be treated like this. Let Father kill himself. I'll kill myself too. This life is a degradation. It would be best to jump over that cliff and have done with it. Serve you all right. I'll get up.

"Fräulein Else . . ."

"Forgive me, Herr von Dorsday, for having troubled you at all in the circumstances. I can perfectly understand your disinclination to concern yourself in the matter."

There, that's done, I'm off.

"Don't go, Fräulein Else."

Don't go? Why shouldn't I go? He's going to give the money. Yes. Not a doubt of it. He must. But I won't sit down again. I'll remain standing, as if it was only for half a second. I'm a little taller than he is.

"You haven't waited for my answer, Else. Once before — pardon me, Else, for referring to it in this connection —" he needn't say Else so often — *"I was able to help your*

father out of a difficulty. Certainly that was a still more absurdly small sum than this time, and I didn't cherish any hope of ever seeing the money again. So there really seems to be no reason for refusing my assistance this time – and especially when a young girl like you, Else, when you yourself come to me as a supplicant –"

What's he driving at? That tone has gone out of his voice. Or it has become different. How he eyes me! He'd better be careful!

"And so, Else, I'm ready ... Dr. Fiala shall have the thirty thousand gulden the day after tomorrow at twelve noon ... on one condition."

I won't let him say any more, I won't!

"Herr von Dorsday, I, I personally guarantee that my father will repay this sum as soon as he has received his fee from Erbesheimer. The Erbesheimers have paid nothing at all so far. Not even an advance ... Mother herself writes –"

"No, don't, Else, one should never undertake a guarantee for another person – not even for one's self."

What does he want? There's that tone in his voice again. Never has anyone eyed me like this! I guess what he's leading up to. He'd better look out!

"Should I have thought it possible an hour ago that I should ever dream of making a condition in such a case? And now I'm doing it. Yes, Else, I'm only a man after all, and it isn't my fault that you are so beautiful, Else ..."

What does he want? What does he want?

47

"Perhaps I should have asked of you today or tomorrow what I ask of you now, even if you had not wanted a million – I beg your pardon, thirty thousand gulden from me. But, of course, if things had been otherwise, you would hardly have given me the opportunity of talking to you alone for so long ..."

"Oh, I have really taken up too much of your time already, Herr von Dorsday."

That was well said. Fred would have approved of that. What's this? He's trying to take hold of my hand? What's he thinking of?

"Haven't you known for a long time, Else? ..."

He must let go of my hand! Thank Heaven, he's let go of it. Not so close, not so close ...

"You wouldn't have been a woman, Else, if you hadn't noticed it. Je vous désire."

He needn't have said that in French – Monsieur le Vicomte!

"Need I say more?"

"You've said too much already, Herr von Dorsday" ... I still stand here. Why? I'll go – I'll go without a word more ...

"Else, Else!" – he's at my side again – *"forgive me, Else. I was only joking too, as you were just now about the million. I too will not put my demand so high – as you feared – I'm sorry to have to put it like that ... so that the smaller demand will perhaps be a pleasant surprise for you. Please don't go, Else."*

And I don't go! Why? Here we stand face to face. Oughtn't I simply to have slapped his face? Haven't I still time to do it now? The two Englishmen are passing. This would be just the minute. Why didn't I do it? I'm a coward, I'm broken, I'm humiliated. What will he want now instead of the million? A kiss, perhaps? That might be discussed. A million is to thirty thousand as ... there are funny comparisons.

"If you really should need a million some day, Else — I'm not a rich man, but we'll see. But this time I will be moderate, like you. And this time I want nothing more, Else, than — to see you."

Is he mad? He does see me. Oh, that's what he means! Why don't I hit him in the face, the swine? Have I turned red or white? You want to see me with nothing on? Many people would like that! I'm pretty with nothing on. Why don't I smack his face? His face is enormous. Why so close, you brute? I don't want your breath on my cheeks. Why don't I simply go? Are his eyes holding me fast? We glare at each other like deadly enemies. I'd like to call him a brute, but I can't. Or won't?

"You look at me as if you thought me mad, Else. Perhaps I am a little mad, for there is a magic in you Else, that you yourself cannot imagine. You must understand, Else, that my request implies no insult. Yes, I say request, although it looks uncommonly like blackmail. But I'm not a blackmailer, I'm

only a man who has had many experiences and has learnt, among other things, that everything in this world has its price, and that anyone who gives away his money when he might get something in return for it is a consummate fool. And the sale of what I want to buy this time, Else, much as it is, will not make you poorer. And I swear to you, Else, by – by all the charms by the revelation of which you would make me happy, that it will remain a secret between you and me."

Where did he learn to talk like that? It sounds like a piece out of a book.

"And I swear to you further that I will not make use of the situation in any way which was not contemplated in our agreement. I ask of you nothing more than to be allowed to stand for a quarter of an hour in reverent contemplation of your beauty. My room is on the same floor as yours, Else, number 65, easy to remember. The Swedish tennis-player you spoke of today was sixty-five, wasn't he?"

He's mad. Why do I let him go on talking? I'm paralysed.

"But if for any reason it doesn't suit you to visit me in room number 65, Else, I propose a little walk after dinner. There's a clearing in the woods – I discovered it by chance the other day – hardly five minutes from the hotel. It would be a wonderful summer night, almost warm, and the starlight will clothe you superbly."

He speaks as he would speak to a female slave. I'd like to spit in his face.

"You need not give your answer at once, Else. Think it over. Please notify me of your decision after dinner."

Why does he say 'notify'? What a stupid word – 'notify.'

"Think it over quietly. Perhaps you'll see that I'm not simply driving a bargain with you ..."

What else are you doing, you blackguard?

"Perhaps you'll realise that it is a man speaking to you, a man who is rather lonely and not particularly happy, and who perhaps deserves a little consideration."

Affected beast! He talks like a bad actor. His manicured fingers look like claws. No, no, I won't! Why don't I tell him so? Kill yourself, Father! What is he doing with my hand? My arm is quite limp. He raises my hand to his lips. Hot lips. Ugh! My hand is cold. I'd like to knock his hat off. Ha, how funny it would be! Will you have done kissing soon, you brute? ... The arc lamps in front of the hotel are lighted already. Two windows on the third floor are open. The one in which the curtain is moving is mine. There's something shining on the wardrobe. There's nothing on the top of it, it's only the brasswork.

"Au revoir then, Else."

I don't answer. I stand here without moving. He looks deeply into my eyes. My face is impenetrable. He knows nothing. He doesn't know whether I'll come or not. I don't know either. I only know that everything's over. I'm half dead. There he goes. He stoops a little. Beast! He feels my look on the back of his neck. Who is he taking off his hat to? Two ladies. He bows as if he were a Count. Paul ought to call him out and shoot him. Or Rudi. What does he think anyhow? Impudent rascal! Never, never! There's nothing for it, Father, you'll have to kill yourself . . .

Those two are obviously coming back from a trip. Both of them nice-looking, he and she. Will they have time to change before dinner? They're on their honeymoon, for certain – or perhaps they're not married at all. I'll never go on a honeymoon. Thirty thousand gulden. No, no, no. Aren't there thirty thousand gulden somewhere in the world? I'll go and see Fiala. I can get there in time. Mercy, mercy, Dr. Fiala. 'With pleasure, my dear young lady. Kindly step into my bedroom.' . . . 'Please, Paul, do me a kindness, ask your father for thirty thousand gulden. Tell him you have gambling debts, that if you don't get the money you must shoot yourself.' 'Gladly, my dear cousin. My room is number so-and-so, I'll expect you at midnight.' Oh, Herr von Dorsday, how moderate you are! For the time being. He's dressing now, putting on a dinner jacket. Now we've got to decide. The meadow by moonlight or room number 65. Will he come into the woods with me in a dinner jacket?

There's still time before dinner. I'll go for a little walk and think the thing over quietly. I'm a lonely old man – ha, ha! Heavenly air, like champagne. It's not cold any longer ... Thirty thousand ... thirty thousand ... I must stand out very prettily in this wide landscape. It's a pity there are no more people out of doors. The man over there near the edge of the wood evidently likes me. Oh, my dear sir, I'm even prettier with nothing on, and it's dirt cheap, thirty thousand gulden. Perhaps you'll bring your friends with you, then it'll be cheaper. Let's hope all your friends are nice-looking – handsomer and younger than Herr von Dorsday. Do you know Herr von Dorsday? He's a beast – a dirty beast ...

Yes, I must think it over. A human life is at stake. Father's life. But no, he won't kill himself, he'd rather go to prison. Three years' penal servitude, or five. He's been living in continual fear of this for five or ten years ... Trust money ... And Mother just as much. And I too ... Who shall I have to undress for next time? Or shall we stick to Herr von Dorsday for simplicity's sake? His present mistress is nothing very grand 'between ourselves.' He'd certainly prefer me. I don't know, I'm not at all sure that I'm much better. Don't put on airs, Fräulein Else, I could tell tales about you ... a certain dream, for instance, that you've had three times now ... and that you haven't told even to your friend Bertha. And she can stand a good deal. And what happened this year at Gmunden, at six in the morning, on the balcony, my proud Fräulein Else? Perhaps you didn't notice the two young men in a boat who were staring at you. Certainly they couldn't make my face out clearly from the lake, but they must have seen that I was in my chemise. And I liked it. Oh, more than liked it. I was intoxicated. I drew my hands across my hips and behaved as if I didn't know anyone was looking at me. And the boat didn't move from the spot. Yes, that's what I am. A hussy. They all see it. Paul sees it. Of course he does, he's a woman's doctor; and the young naval officer saw it too, and so did the painter. Only Fred doesn't see it, the silly boy. That's why he loves me. But I wouldn't like to be naked in front of him – no, never, never! I wouldn't like it at all. I'd be ashamed. But before the rogue with the Roman head – rather! Best of all before him! Even if I had to die the next minute. But one needn't die the next minute. One survives it. Bertha has survived more than that.

No, no, I won't! I'll go to anyone else – but not to him. To Paul, if you like. Or I'll choose somebody for myself tonight at dinner. It's all the same. But I can't tell everyone that I want thirty thousand gulden in return. That would be like a woman from the Kärntnerstrasse. No, I won't sell myself. Never. I'll never sell myself. I'll give myself. Yes, if once I find the right man, I'll give myself. But I won't sell myself. I'll be a hussy, but not a prostitute. You have miscalculated, Herr von Dorsday. And so has Father. Yes, he has miscalculated. He must have foreseen it. He knows men. He knows Herr von Dorsday. He must have known that Herr Dorsday wouldn't give something for absolutely nothing. Otherwise he could have telegraphed, or come here himself. But this way was more comfortable and safer, wasn't it, Father? When a man has a pretty daughter, why need he go to prison? And Mother, stupid as ever, sits down and writes the letter. Father didn't trust himself to do it. If he had written, I should have noticed at once that something was up. But you won't succeed. No, you speculated too certainly on my childish affection, Father, you assumed too certainly that I'd rather undergo any indignity than let you bear the consequences of your criminal frivolity. You're a genius. Herr von Dorsday says it, everybody says it. But how does that help me? Fiala's a nobody, but he doesn't embezzle trust money. Even Waldheim isn't to be mentioned in the same breath as you … Who said that? Dr. Froriep. 'Your Father is a genius.' And I've only heard him speak once! Last year at the assizes … For the first

and last time. It was glorious. Tears ran down my
cheeks. And the poor wretch he was defending was
acquitted. Perhaps he wasn't such a poor wretch. At
any rate he had only stolen, he hadn't misappropriated trust money to play baccarat and speculate on
the Bourse. Now Father himself will stand before the
jury. It will be in all the papers. Second day of the
trial, third day of the trial; counsel for the defence
rose to reply. Who will defend him? Not a genius.
Nothing will help him. Unanimous verdict of guilty.
Sentenced to five years. Stones, convict's clothes,
cropped hair. Visitors allowed once a month. I go
there with Mother, third class. We have no money.
No one lends us anything. A little flat in the
Lerchenfelderstrasse, like the one where I went to
see the seamstress ten years ago. We take him some
food. From where? For we have nothing ourselves.
Uncle Victor will makes us an allowance. Three
hundred gulden a month. Rudi will be in Holland at
Vanderhulst's, if they're still willing to take him. The
Convict's Children. Three-volume novel by Temme.
Father receives us in striped convict's clothes. He
doesn't look angry, only sad. He simply can't look
angry. 'Else, if you had got me the money that time.'
That's what he'll think, but he won't say anything.
He won't have the heart to reproach me. He's kind-
hearted – but he's careless. His weakness is his pas-

sion for gambling. He can't help it, it's a kind of insanity. Perhaps they'll acquit him on the ground of insanity.

And he didn't give enough thought to the letter. Perhaps it never occurred to him that Dorsday would take advantage of the situation and ask such an indignity of me. He's a good friend of our family, he lent Father eight thousand gulden once before. How should one suspect that a man would act in such a way? Father tried everything else first, for certain. What he must have gone through before ' made Mother write this letter! He must ha from one person to another, from W Burin, from Burin to Wertheimstein, knows to whom next. He's sure to hav Uncle Carl too. And they all left him in t All his so-called friends. And now Dorsda hope, his last hope. And if the money doesn he'll kill himself. Of course he'll kill himse won't let them send him to prison. Arrest, assizes, prison, convict's clothes! No, no! When warrant comes, he'll shoot himself or hang himself. He'll hang himself from the window bar. They'll send word to us from the house opposite. The locksmith will have to open the door, and it will have been my fault. And now he's sitting with Mother in the very room where he's going to hang himself the

day after tomorrow, smoking a Havana cigar. Where
does he still get Havana cigars from? I can hear him
speaking, hear how he quiets Mother. 'You can be
sure Dorsday will send the money. Remember, I
saved him a big sum last winter through my inter-
vention. And now the Erbesheimer case is coming
on ...' Really ... I hear him speaking. Telepathy!
Remarkable. I see Fred too at this very moment.
He's passing the casino in the Stadtpark with a girl.
She's wearing a pale-blue blouse and light-coloured
shoes and she's rather hoarse. I know it all quite positively. When I get to Vienna I'll ask Fred whether
he was in the Stadtpark with his sweetheart on the
3rd of September between seven and eight in the
evening ...

Where shall I go now? What's the matter with me?
It's quite dark, almost. How lovely and quiet. Not a
soul to be seen anywhere. They're all at dinner by
now. Telepathy? No, that isn't telepathy. I heard the
gong a little while ago. 'Where's Else?' Paul will
think? They'll all notice if I'm not there for the hors
d'oeuvres. They'll send up for me. 'What's wrong
with Else? She's always so punctual.' The two men
by the window will think, 'Where's the pretty little
girl with the reddish blonde hair today?' And Herr
von Dorsday will be frightened. He is certainly a
coward. Don't worry Herr von Dorsday, nothing

will happen to you. I despise you so utterly. If I wished it, you'd be a dead man tomorrow evening. I'm sure Paul would call him out if I told him the story. I make you a present of your life, Herr von Dorsday.

How immensely broad the meadows are, and how huge and black the mountains. There are hardly any stars. Yes there are, three, four — there'll soon be more. And the wood behind me. It's pleasant to sit here on the seat at the edge of the wood. The hotel is so far, far away, and the lights are like the lights of fairyland. And what brutes live in it! Oh no — people, poor people; I am so sorry for them all. I'm even sorry for the Marchesa, I don't know why, and Frau Winawer and Cissy's little girl's nurse. She doesn't come to the table d'hôte, she has had her dinner earlier with Fritzi. 'What's this about Else?' Cissy asks. 'What? isn't she in her room either?' They're all worried about me, I know. I'm the only person who isn't worried. Yes, here I am at Martino di Castrozza, sitting on a seat at the edge of the wood, and the air is like champagne, and I think I'm crying. Yes, and why am I crying? There's nothing to cry about. It's nerves. I must control myself. I mustn't let myself go like this. But crying isn't at all unpleasant. Crying always does me good. When I went to see our old French nurse in hospital — she died afterwards – I cried. And at Grandmamma's funeral, and when Bertha went to Nuremberg, and when Agatha's baby died, and when we saw *La Dame aux Camélias* at the theatre – I cried then, too. Who'll cry when I'm dead? ...

Oh, how lovely it would be to be dead! I lie on a bier in the drawing-room, with candles burning. Long candles. Twelve long candles. The hearse is at the door already. People are standing outside. How old was she? Only nineteen. Really only nineteen? Think of it, her father is in prison. Why did she kill herself? From unrequited love for a rascal. What are you talking about? She was going to have a baby. No, she fell from the Cimone. It was an accident. Good day, Herr von Dorsday, are you too doing the last honour to little Else? Little Else, the old woman says. Why? Of course I must do her the last honour, it was I who did her the first dishonour. Oh, it was worth the trouble, Frau Winawer. I've never seen such a beautiful body. It cost me only thirty million. A Rubens costs three times as much. She poisoned herself with hashish. She only wanted to have beautiful visions, but she took too much and never woke up again. Why is Herr von Dorsday wearing a red monocle? Who is he waving to with his handkerchief? Mother comes down the steps and kisses his hand. Shame, shame. Now they are whispering to each other. I can't understand a word, because I'm on a bier. The wreath of violets round my forehead is from Paul. The ribbons hang down to the floor. No one dares to come into the room. I'd like to get up and look out of the window. What a great blue lake! A hundred ships with yellow sails. The waves glisten. So much sun. A regatta. The men are wearing rowing shorts. The ladies are in bathing dresses. It's not decent. They imagine I'm naked. How stupid they are, I'm wearing mourning because I'm dead. I'll prove it to you. I'll lie down on the bier again at once. Where is it? It's gone. They've carried it away. They've embezzled it. That's why Father's in prison. And they've acquitted him for three years. The jury are all bribed by Fiala. Now I'll walk to the cemetery, that'll save Mother the funeral expenses. We must economise. I'm walking so fast that no one follows me. Oh, how fast I can walk. They all stand in the streets and marvel. How can they look like that at someone who's dead? It's impertinent. I would rather go across the fields; they're all blue with forget-me-nots and violets. The naval officers stand in a double line. Good morning, gentlemen. Open the gate, champion. Don't you recognise me? I'm the corpse. But you needn't kiss my hand on that account. Where's my tomb? Have they embezzled that too? Thank God, it's not the cemetery after

all. It's the park at Menton. Father'll be glad that
I'm not buried. I'm not afraid of snakes. If only one
doesn't bite my foot. Oh dear! ...

What's happened? Where am I? Have I been
asleep? Yes, I've been asleep. I must have been
dreaming. My feet are so cold. My right foot's cold.
Why? There's a little tear in the stocking, on the
ankle. Why am I still sitting in the wood? They must
have sounded the gong for dinner long ago.

Oh Lord, where was I? I was so far away! What
was I dreaming about? I think I was dead. And I
had no worries and didn't have to rack my brains.
Thirty thousand, thirty thousand ... I haven't got
them yet. I must earn them first. And here I am sitting alone on the edge of the wood. The hotel lights
are shining. I must go back. But there's no time to
be lost. Herr von Dorsday is waiting for my decision.
Decision. Decision! No. No, Herr von Dorsday, once
and for all, No. You were joking, of course, Herr
von Dorsday. Yes, that's what I'll say to him. Oh,
that's excellent! Your joke wasn't a very delicate one,
Herr von Dorsday, but I'll forgive you. I'll telegraph
to Father tomorrow morning, Herr von Dorsday,
that the money will be in Dr. Fiala's hands at the
appointed time. Wonderful. That's what I'll say to

him. He'll have no choice; he must send the money. Must? Must he? Why must he? And if he did, he'd revenge himself somehow. He'd arrange it so that the money arrived too late. Or he'd send the money and then tell everybody that I had sold myself to him. But he won't send the money at all. 'No, Fräulein Else, that wasn't our bargain. Telegraph what you like to your father, I shall not send the money. You needn't think, Fräulein Else, that I shall let myself be made a fool of by a little girl like you – I, the Vicomte d'Eperies.'

I must walk carefully. The road is quite dark. It's curious, but I feel better than I did. Nothing at all has changed, and I feel better. What was I dreaming about? About a champion? What sort of a champion? It's farther to the hotel than I thought. They're all sure to be still at dinner. I'll sit down quietly at the table, say I've had a bad headache and have my dinner brought afterwards. Herr von Dorsday will come to me of his own accord and say that the whole thing was only a joke. Forgive me, Fräulein Else, for my bad joke. I've telegraphed to my bank already. But he won't say it. He hasn't telegraphed. Everything is exactly as it was before. He's waiting. Herr von Dorsday is waiting. No, I won't see him. I can't see him any more. I won't see anyone any more. I won't go back to the hotel, I

won't go home. I won't go to Vienna, I won't go to
anybody, to anyone at all, not to Father, not to
Mother, not to Rudi, not to Fred, not to Bertha, not
to Aunt Irene! She's the best of them, she'd understand everything. But I've nothing more to do with
her or with anybody else. If I were a magician, I'd
be in quite another part of the world. On some
splendid ship in the Mediterranean, but not alone.
With Paul, perhaps. Yes, I can imagine that quite
easily. Or I'd live in a villa by the sea and we'd lie
on the marble steps that run down into the water,
and he'd hold me tight in his arms and bite my lips,
as Albert did at the piano two years ago, the impudent wretch. No. I'd lie alone on the marble steps by
the sea and wait. And at last a man would come, or
several men, and I'd choose one, and the others
whom I had rejected would throw themselves into the
sea in despair. Or they'd have to be patient and wait
till next day. Oh, what a delicious life it would be!

What have my beautiful shoulders and my pretty
slender legs been given me for? Why do I exist at
all? And it would serve them right, all of them,
they've brought me up to sell myself in one way or
another. They wouldn't hear of my going on the
stage. They laughed at me. It would have served
them quite right last year if I'd married Director
Wilomitzer, who's close on fifty. Not that they didn't

try to persuade me. Father certainly drew the line at that, but Mother dropped some very plain hints.

How huge the hotel is. Like a monstrous, illuminated magic castle. Everything is gigantic. The mountains, too. Terrifyingly gigantic. They've never been so black before. The moon hasn't risen yet. It'll rise just in time for the performance, the great performance in the meadow, when Herr von Dorsday makes his female slave dance naked. What's Herr von Dorsday to me? Now, Mademoiselle Else, what are you making such a fuss about? You were ready to go off and be the mistress of strange men, one after the other. And you boggle at the trifle which Herr von Dorsday asks of you? You're ready to sell yourself for a pearl necklace, for beautiful clothes, for a villa by the sea? And your father's life isn't worth as much as that? It would be just the right start. It would justify all the rest at once. It was you, I could say, you brought me to it. You're all to blame for my having become what I am, not Father and Mother only, but Rudi too, and Fred and everybody, because no one troubles about me. A little tenderness when you look pretty, a little anxiety when you've got a temperature, and they send you to school and you have piano lessons and French lessons at home, and you go to the country in the summer and you get presents on your birthday and they talk about all sorts of things at dinner. But what I feel – my secret trouble, my secret fears – have you ever thought of them? Sometimes there was a trace of it in Father's eyes, but it passed away quickly. And the next moment he was thinking of his practice again and his worries and speculations, and probably some woman in the background, 'nothing very grand between ourselves' ... and I was alone again. Well, what would you do, Father, what would you do today if I wasn't here?

Here I am in front of the hotel ... How awful to have to go in and see all the people – Herr von Dorsday, my aunt, Cissy. How pleasant it was just now on the seat at the edge of the wood when I was dead. A champion ... If only I could remember what it was all about ... It was a regatta, that's right, and I was watching it from the window. But who was the champion? ... Oh, if only I wasn't so tired, so awfully tired. And now, have I got to sit up till midnight and then creep into Herr von Dorsday's room? Perhaps I'll meet Cissy in the passage ... Oughtn't I to ask Cissy for advice? It's so hard for a beginner! Of course I mustn't tell her that it's Dorsday. I'd rather she thought I had a rendezvous with one of the good-looking young men in the hotel. For example, the tall fair man with the bright

eyes. But he's gone. He suddenly disappeared. I
never even thought of him till this minute. But it's
not the tall fair man with the bright eyes, worse luck,
it's not even Paul, it's Herr von Dorsday. How shall
I manage it? What shall I say to him? Just yes? But I
can't go to Herr von Dorsday's room. I'm sure he's
got all kinds of beautiful bottles on his washstand,
and the room always smells of French scent. No, I
wouldn't go to his room for the whole world. I'd
rather it was in the open air. He won't trouble me
there. The sky is so high and the meadow so big. I
mustn't think of Herr Dorsday at all. I mustn't even
look at him. And if he dares to touch me I'll kick
him with my bare feet. Oh, if only it were someone
else, anyone else. He could have everything, everything he wanted of me tonight, that other one – only
not Dorsday. Oh, that it should be him! just him!
How his eyes will stab and drill their way into me.
He'll stand there with his monocle and grin. No, he
won't grin. He'll put on a dignified expression. For
he's used to this sort of thing. How many girls has
he seen – like that? A hundred, a thousand? But was
there one among them like me. No, certainly there
wasn't. I'll tell him he's not the first who's seen me
like that. I'll tell him I've got a lover – but only after
the thirty thousand gulden have been sent to Fiala.
Then I'll tell him he's a fool – that he could have

had anything he wanted of me for the same money. That I've had ten lovers already, twenty, a hundred ... But he won't believe a word of it ... And if he does believe it, what good will it do me? ...

If only I could spoil his pleasure somehow! Suppose someone else was there! Why not? He did not say that he must be alone with me. Oh, Herr von Dorsday, I'm so afraid of you. Won't you kindly allow me to bring a good friend with me? Oh, that's not in any way contrary to the agreement, Herr von Dorsday. If I liked I could invite the whole hotel, and you'd still be bound to send the thirty thousand gulden. But I'll content myself with bringing my Cousin Paul. Or would you prefer someone else. The tall fair man has gone, unfortunately, and so has the rogue with the Roman head. But I'll find someone else. You're afraid of an indiscretion. That doesn't matter. I don't care a straw about discretion. When one has gone as far as I have, nothing matters. Today is only a beginning. Or do you think that I shall go home from this adventure as a respectable girl of good family? No, neither good family nor respectable young girl. There'll be an end to that once for all. Hereafter I stand on my own two feet. I have pretty legs, as you and the other participants in the festivity will soon have an opportunity of perceiving. So that's settled, Herr von

Dorsday. At ten o'clock, when all the others are sitting in the lounge, we'll walk across the meadows in the moonlight, through the woods to the famous clearing discovered by yourself. You will bring the telegram to the bank with you in case of eventualities. For I'm entitled to ask for a guarantee from a rogue like you. And at midnight you can go home again, and I'll stay in the meadow in the moonlight with my cousin or someone else. You've no objection to that, Herr von Dorsday? You can't have. And if by any chance I should be found dead tomorrow morning, don't be surprised. In that case Paul will send the telegram. I shall have seen to that.

But don't imagine, for Heaven's sake, that you, a miserable creature like you, have driven me to my death. I've known for a long time that I'd end up like this. Just ask my friend Fred if I haven't often said so to him. Fred, he's Herr Friedrich Wenkheim – the only respectable person, by the way, I've ever known in my life. The only one I could have loved, if he hadn't been so respectable. Yes, I'm a depraved creature. I wasn't made for a bourgeois existence, and I've no talent. Perhaps it would be best for our family if it died out. There'll be a catastrophe of some kind with Rudi. He'll get into debt over a Dutch music-hall singer and defraud Vanderhulst. It runs in the family. My father's youngest brother shot himself when he was fifteen. No one knows why. I didn't know him. Ask them to show you his photograph, Herr von Dorsday. We have it in an album ... I'm supposed to be like him. Nobody knows why he killed himself. And nobody will know why I did. It wasn't on your account anyhow, Herr von Dorsday. I won't do you that honour. At nineteen or twenty-one – it's all the same. Or shall I become a nurse or a telephone operator or marry a Herr Wilomitzer or let you keep me? It's all equally disgusting, and I won't go to the meadow with you at all. No, it's all too tiring and too stupid and too unpleasant. When I'm dead, will you be kind enough to send the few thousand gulden to Father, because it certainly would be too sad if he were arrested on the very day that my body was taken to Vienna. But I'll leave a letter with a testamentary disposition. Herr von Dorsday shall have the right to see my body, my beautiful, naked maiden body. So you can't complain, Herr von Dorsday, that I have deceived you. You're getting something for your money. There's nothing in our contract about my still being alive. Oh no. It's not in writing anywhere. Well then – I bequeath a view of my body to the art dealer Dorsday, and I bequeath to Herr Fred Wenkheim my diary of my seventeenth year – I haven't written any more – and I bequeath to

Cissy's Fräulein the five twenty-franc pieces which I brought from Switzerland years ago. They're in the writing-table drawer with the letters. And I bequeath to Bertha my black evening dress. And to Agatha my books. And to Cousin Paul – to him I bequeath a kiss on my pale lips. And to Cissy I bequeath my tennis racket, because I'm generous. And I'm to be buried here at San Martino di Castrozza, in the pretty little cemetery. I don't want to go home again. I won't go home again even as a corpse. And Father and Mother mustn't grieve, I'm better off than they are. And I forgive them. I'm not to be pitied ... Ha, ha, what a funny will! I'm really moved to think that I shall be dead by this time to-morrow, when the others are at dinner ... Aunt Emma won't go down to dinner, of course, nor will Paul. They'll have their meals sent up to their rooms. I'm curious to know how Cissy will behave. Only, unfortunately, I shan't know. I shan't know anything more. Or perhaps one knows everything so long as one isn't buried. And after all, I'm only pretending to be dead. And if Herr von Dorsday comes near my corpse, I'll wake up and open my eyes, and he'll be so frightened that he'll drop his monocle.

But none of it's true, worse luck! I shan't be pretending to be dead, or really dead. I shan't kill myself at all, I'm much too cowardly. I may be a plucky climber, but I'm a coward all the same. And perhaps I haven't even got enough veronal. How many powders does one have to take? Six, I think. But ten are safer. I think there are ten left. Yes, that'll be enough.

How many times have I walked round the hotel? And what now? I'm outside the door. There's no one in the lounge. Of course not – they're all still at dinner. The lounge looks strange with no one at all there. There's a hat on that chair, a tourist's hat, very smart. A pretty chamois beard. There's an old gentleman sitting in an armchair. Probably he hasn't any appetite. Reading the paper. He's well off. He hasn't any worries. He's reading his paper quietly, and I have to rack my brains to get thirty thousand gulden for Father. No. I know how. It's so terribly simple. What am I doing? What am I doing here in the lounge? They'll all be coming from dinner in a minute. What shall I do? Herr von Dorsday's certainly sitting on pins. Where is she, he's thinking. Has she killed herself? Or is she hiring someone to kill me? Or is she setting her Cousin Paul on me? Don't be afraid, Herr von Dorsday, I'm not such a dangerous person. I'm a little hussy, nothing more. You shall be rewarded for the anxiety you have endured. Twelve o'clock, room number 65. It would be too chilly out of doors after all. And from your room,

Herr von Dorsday, I shall go straight to my Cousin
Paul. You don't object to that, Herr von Dorsday?

"Else! Else!"

What? That's Paul's voice. Is dinner over already?

"Else!"

"Oh, Paul. Why, what's the matter, Paul?" ... I'll put
on an innocent air.

"Where have you been hiding, Else?"

*"Where do you suppose I've been hiding? I've been for a
walk."*

"Now — during dinner?"

"Well, why not? After all, it's the best time for it." I'm
talking nonsense.

*"Mother has been imagining all sorts of things. I went to
your door and knocked."*

"I didn't hear you."

*"But seriously, Else, how can you make us so uneasy? At
least you could have let Mother know that you weren't coming
down to dinner."*

*"You're right, Paul, but if you'd had any idea what a
headache I've had."*

I talk in a melting voice. Oh, what a hussy I am!

"Are you better now, at any rate?"

"Honestly I couldn't say I am."

"Well, first of all, I'll tell Mother —"

"Stop, Paul, not yet. Apologise to Aunt Emma for me, and

73

I'll just go to my room for a few minutes to make myself tidy. Then I'll come straight down and have something brought to me."

"You're so pale, Else. Shall I send Mother up to you?"

"Don't make so much fuss about me, Paul, and don't look at me like that. Haven't you ever seen a female with a headache? Of course I'll come down. In ten minutes at the longest. Goodbye Paul."

"Au revoir, Else."

Thank Heaven's he's going. A silly boy – but a dear. What does the porter want? What – a telegram? ...

"Thank you. When did the telegram come?"

"A quarter of an hour ago, Fräulein."

Why does he look at me so – compassionately? In Heaven's name, what can be in it? I won't open it till I'm upstairs, or perhaps I'll faint. Probably Father has – if Father's dead, then everything's all right, then I needn't go to the meadow with Herr von Dorsday ... Oh, what a miserable creature I am! Dear God, please let there be nothing bad in the telegram. Dear God, please let Father be alive. Arrested, if you like, but not dead. If there's no bad news in it, I'll offer a sacrifice. I'll become a nurse. I'll go into an office. Don't be dead, father. I'll do everything you want ...

Thank Heaven, I'm upstairs. Turn on the light,

turn on the light. It's got cold. The window's been open too long. Courage, courage. Perhaps it's to say the matter has been settled. Perhaps Uncle Bernhard has given the money, and they're wiring me 'Don't speak to Dorsday.' I'll know in a minute. But if I look at the ceiling I can't read what's in the telegram. Trala, trala, courage. It must be done.

"Implore you again speak Dorsday. Sum not thirty but fifty. Otherwise everything unavailing. Address still Fiala."

... but fifty. Otherwise everything unavailing. Trala, trala! Address still Fiala. Fifty. But surely fifty or thirty makes no difference once way or the other. Not even to Herr von Dorsday. The veronal is under my linen – for an emergency. Why didn't I say fifty in the first place? I thought of it! Otherwise everything unavailing. Well, downstairs at once! I can't stay here sitting on the bed ... 'Excuse me, Herr von Dorsday, a little mistake. Not thirty, but fifty, otherwise everything unavailing. Address still Fiala.' 'Do you take me for a fool, Fräulein Else?' 'Not at all, Monsieur le Vicomte. Why should I?' 'But for fifty I should have to ask correspondingly more, Fräulein.' ... Otherwise everything still unavailing, address still Fiala ... 'As you wish, Herr von Dorsday. Pray command me. But first of all write the telegram to your bank, of course, otherwise I have no security.'

Yes, that's how I'll do it. I'll go to his room and I won't undress till he's written out the telegram before my eyes. And I'll hold the telegram in my hand. Oh, how disgusting! And where shall I put my clothes? No, no, I'll undress here and put on my big black coat, which covers me completely. That'll be the simplest way. For both parties. Address still Fiala. My teeth are chattering. The window's still open. Shut it. In the open air? I might have died of it. Beast! Fifty thousand. He can't say no. Room number 65. But I'll tell Paul beforehand to wait for me in his room. Then I'll go straight from Dorsday to Paul and tell him everything. And then Paul will box his ears. Yes, this very night. It'll be a full programme. And then comes the veronal. No – why? Why die? Not a bit of it. Be merry, be merry, life's only beginning now. You shall have your share of it. You'll be proud of your little daughter. I'll become such a baggage as the world has never seen. Address still Fiala. You shall have your fifty thousand gulden, Father. But with the next money I earn I'll buy myself new nightgowns, with lace, quite transparent, and lovely silk stockings. One only lives once. Why do people look like I do? Light on ... I'll turn on the light over the mirror. How pretty my reddish blonde hair is, and my shoulders; and my eyes aren't bad either. Oh, how big they are. It'd be a pity. There's plenty of time to take veronal.

But I must go down. Right down. Herr Dorsday is waiting, and he doesn't even know yet that the price has become fifty thousand since he saw me. Yes, I've gone up in price, Herr von Dorsday. I must show him the telegram, or he won't believe me; he'll think I'm trying to bring off a business deal. I'll send the telegram to his room and write something to go with it ... 'To my great regret it has become fifty thousand, Herr von Dorsday, but I am sure it is all the same to you. And I am convinced that your counter-proposal was not meant seriously at all. For you are a Vicomte and a gentleman. Tomorrow morning you will send the fifty thousand on which my father's life hangs to Fiala without delay. I count on it.' ... 'Of course, my dear young lady, I'll send a hundred thousand immediately to cover any further contingencies, without asking for anything in return, and I pledge myself furthermore to provide for your whole family from this day forward, to pay your father's Bourse debts and replace all the misappropriated trust money.' Address still Fiala. Ha, ha, ha! Yes, that's just like the Vicomte d'Eperies. But that's all nonsense. What choice have I? It must be. I must do it. I must do everything, everything that Herr von Dorsday asks so that Father may have the money tomorrow, so that he shan't be put in prison, so that he shan't kill himself. And I will do it, too. Yes, I'll do it, although it's all for nothing. In six months we shall be where we are today again! In a month! ... But then it will make no difference to me. I'll make this one sacrifice ... and then no more. Never, never, never more. Yes, I'll tell Father so as soon as I get to Vienna; then out of the house – anywhere. I'll consult Fred. He's the only person who really cares for me. But I've not got as far as that yet. I'm not in Vienna, I'm still at Martino di Castrozza. Nothing has happened yet.

What shall I do then? There's the telegram. What shall I do with the telegram? I knew just now. I must send it to his room. But what else? I must write him something to go with it. Yes, but what shall I write to him? Expect me at twelve. No, no, no! He shall not have his triumph. I won't, I won't, I won't. Thank God I've got the powders. That's the only way out. Where are they? Heavens, they haven't been stolen! No, here they are. Here in the box. Are they all still there? Yes, here they are. One, two, three, four, five, six. I only want to look at them, my dear powders. It commits me to nothing. And pouring them into the glass commits me to nothing. One, two ... but I'm sure I shan't kill myself. I haven't the slightest intention of doing so. Three, four, five ... nothing like enough to kill one. It would be terrible if I hadn't got the veronal with me. Then I'd have to jump out of the window, and I certainly shouldn't have the courage to do that. But veronal ... you go to sleep slowly and never wake up again; no trouble, no pain. You lie in bed, drink it at a draught, dream, and it's all over. The day before yesterday I took a powder, and a few days ago I even took two. Ssh, don't tell anybody. Tonight it'll be a little more. It's only for emergencies. In case I should find it too horrible. But why should I find it horrible? If he touches me, I'll spit in his face. Quite simple.

But how shall I get the letter to him? I can't send a letter to Herr von Dorsday by the chambermaid. It would be best if I went downstairs and talked to him and showed him the telegram. In any case I must go down. I can't stay up here in my room. I couldn't stand it for three hours ... until the moment arrives. I must go down, too, for my aunt's sake. Ha, what is my aunt to me? What are the people to me? Look, ladies and gentlemen, here's the glass of veronal. Now I take it in my hand. Now I raise it to my lips. Yes, at any moment I can be where there are no aunts and no Dorsday and no father who misappropriates trust money ...

But I won't kill myself. I don't need to. And I won't go to Herr von Dorsday's room. I wouldn't dream of it. I'm hanged if for fifty thousand gulden I'll stand naked in front of an old rake just to keep a

rascal out of the dock. No – it must be one thing or
the other. How does Herr von Dorsday come into
it? Must it be Herr von Dorsday? If one sees me,
others shall see me. Yes! ... Splendid idea! Everyone
shall see me. The whole world shall see me. And
then comes the veronal. No, not the veronal – why
should it? – next will come the villa with the marble
steps and the handsome young men and freedom
and the wide world! Good evening, Fräulein Else, I
like you like that. Ha, ha, down there they'll think
I've gone mad. But I've never been so sane. I'm
really sane for the first time in my life. They shall all
see me, all! ... Then there'll be no retreat, no going
home to Father and Mother and uncles and aunts.
Then I shall no longer be the Fräulein Else whom
they'd like to marry off to some Director Wilomitzer;
I'll make fools of them all ... especially that swine
Dorsday ... and come into the world for a second
time ... Otherwise everything unavailing ... address
still Fiala. Ha, ha!

Don't lose any more time, don't become cowardly
again. Off with the dress. Who'll be the first? Will it
be you, Cousin Paul? Lucky for you that the Roman
head has gone. Oh, how beautiful I am! Bertha has a
black silk chemise. Exquisite. I'll be much more
exquisite. Splendid life. Off with the stockings, that
would be indecent. Naked, quite naked. How Cissy

will envy me! And others too. But they don't dare.
They'd all like to so much. Take me as an example.
I, the maiden, I dare. I'll laugh myself to death over
Dorsday. Here I am, Herr von Dorsday. To the post-
office, quick. Fifty thousand. Surely it's worth that?

How beautiful, how beautiful I am! Behold me,
Night! Mountains, behold me! Sky, behold me – see
how beautiful I am! But you're all blind. What do I
get from you? The people downstairs have eyes.
Shall I let down my hair? No. I'd look like a mad
woman. But you mustn't think me mad. You must
only think me shameless. *Canaille.* Where's the
telegram? In Heaven's name, what have I done with
the telegram? There it is lying peacefully by the
veronal. 'I implore you again ... fifty thousand ...
otherwise everything unavailing. Address still Fiala.'
Yes, that's how the telegram goes. That's a piece of
paper and there are words on it. Handed in in
Vienna at 4.30. No; I'm not dreaming, it's all true.
And at home they're all waiting for the fifty thousand gulden, and Herr von Dorsday is waiting too.
Let him wait. There's plenty of time. Oh, how nice
it is to walk up and down the room like this with
nothing on. Am I really as pretty as I look in that
mirror? Oh, won't you come closer, pretty Fräulein?
I want to kiss your blood-red lips. What a pity the
glass is between us, the cold glass. How well we

should get on together. Shouldn't we? We should not want anyone else. Perhaps there are no other people. There are telegrams and hotels and mountains and railway stations and woods, but there are no people. We only dream them. Only Dr. Fiala exists, with the address. It's still the same. Oh, I'm not at all mad. I'm only a little excited. That's quite natural, when one is just going to come into the world for a second time. For the old Else is dead already. Yes, most certainly I'm dead. There's no veronal needed. Shan't I pour it away? The chambermaid might drink it by mistake. I'll leave a bit of paper there and write 'Poison' on it; no, 'Medicine' ... so that nothing shall happen to the chambermaid. I'm so magnanimous! There, 'Medicine,' underlined twice, and three exclamation marks. Now nothing can happen. And if I come upstairs and don't want to kill myself, and only want to sleep, I won't drink the whole glass, but only a quarter of it, or perhaps even less. Quite simple.

Everything's ready. It would be simplest to run down, along the passages and downstairs, just as I am. No – I might be stopped before I got down ... and I must be sure that Herr von Dorsday will be there. Otherwise, of course, he won't send the money off – the swine ... But I've still got to write to him. That's the most important thing of all. Oh,

how cold the back of the chair is, but it's pleasant.
When I've got my villa on the Italian Lakes I shall
always walk in my park with nothing on ... I'll leave
my fountain pen to Fred when I die. But for the
moment I've something more sensible to do than to
die ... 'Most honoured Monsieur le Vicomte' ...
Don't be silly, Else, no introduction, neither most
honoured nor most despised. 'Your condition, Herr
von Dorsday, is fulfilled' ... 'At the moment when
you read these lines, Herr von Dorsday, your condition is fulfilled, although perhaps not quite in the
way you had anticipated' ... 'Why, how well the girl
writes,' Father would say ... 'And so I assume that
you on your side will keep your word, and send the
fifty thousand gulden immediately by telegraph to
the address you know. Else.' ... No, not Else. No
signature at all. There. My pretty yellow writing
paper! I got it at Christmas. Too bad. There – and
now the telegram and letter go into the envelope ...
'Herr von Dorsday, Room No. 65.' Why the number? I'll just put the letter outside his door as I go
by. But I needn't, I needn't do anything. If I like, I
can get in to bed now and go to sleep and not worry
about anything any more. Not about Herr von
Dorsday and not about Father. A striped convict's
dress is really quite stylish, and lots of people have
shot themselves. And we must all die.

But you needn't do anything of the sort for the time being, Father. You've got your splendidly developed daughter, and the address is still Fiala. I'll start a collection. I'll go round with the plate. Why should only Herr von Dorsday pay? That would be unfair. Everyone according to his means. How much will Paul put in the plate? How much will the man with the gold pince-nez put in? But don't imagine that the fun will last long. I shall soon cover myself up again, run upstairs to my room, lock myself in, and if I want to, drink the whole glass at one draught. But I shan't want to. It would be an act of cowardice. They don't deserve so much respect, the brutes. Ashamed to look you in the face? Not at all. Let me look into your eyes once more, lovely Else. What huge eyes you've got, when one comes close to you. I wish someone would kiss me on my eyes, on my blood-red mouth. My coat hardly covers my ankles. They'll notice that my feet are bare. What does it matter? They'll see more! But I'm not bound to do it. I can turn back at once, before I get downstairs. I can turn back on the first floor. I needn't go down at all. But I will. I'm glad to do it. Haven't I wanted something like this all my life?

What am I waiting for? I'm ready. The performance can begin. But don't forget the letter. An aristocratic handwriting, Fred declares. Au revoir, Else.

You're pretty in your coat. Florentine ladies had themselves painted like that. Their portraits are hung in galleries, and it's an honour for them. People won't notice anything when I've got the coat on. Only my feet, only my feet. I'll put on my black patent leather shoes, then they'll think I'm wearing flesh-coloured stockings. I'll walk through the lounge, and nobody'll suspect that there's nothing under the coat but me, just me. And then I can always come upstairs again ... Who's playing the piano so nicely down there? Chopin? ... Herr von Dorsday must be rather nervous. Perhaps he's afraid of Paul. Only patience, patience, everything will arrange itself. I don't know anything yet, Herr von Dorsday. I'm in terrible suspense myself. Turn out the light. Is everything in the room right? Goodbye, veronal, au revoir. Goodbye, my passionately loved image. How you shine in the darkness! I'm quite used to having nothing on under the coat already. Quite pleasant. Who knows if there aren't a lot of people sitting in the lounge like this without anyone knowing it? Perhaps lots of women go to the theatre and sit in their boxes like this – for fun or for other reasons.

Shall I lock the door? Why? There's no stealing here. And if there were ... I don't want anything any more. Finished ... Where's number 65? There's no one in the passage. They're all still at dinner downstairs. 61 ... 62 ... what huge mountain boots outside the door. There's a pair of trousers hanging on the hook. How indecent. 64, 65. So that's where the Vicomte lives ... I'll lean the letter against the door. He can't help seeing it there. Nobody'll steal it? Well, there it is ... It makes no difference ... I can still do as I like. I fancy I've made a fool of him ... If only I don't meet him on the stairs now. Here he comes ... No, it's not him! ... This man is much better-looking than Herr von Dorsday, very stylish, with a little black moustache. When did he come? I might have a little rehearsal ... lift the coat just a tiny bit. I should so much like to. Just look at me, sir. You've no idea whom you're passing. It's a pity you've got to go upstairs just now. Why don't you stay in the lounge? You're missing something. Great performance. Why don't you stop me? My fate lies in your hands. If you speak to me, I'll turn back. So please speak to me. I'm looking at you so kindly ... He doesn't speak. He's past. He's turning round, I feel it. Call, speak! Save me! Perhaps, sir, you will be to blame for my death. But you'll never know it.

Where am I? In the lounge so soon. How did I get here? So few people and so many strangers. Or is my eyesight bad? Where's Dorsday? He isn't here. Is it the hand of Providence? I'll go back. I'll write another letter to Dorsday. I expect you in my room at midnight. Bring the telegram to your bank with you. No. He might think it was a trap. It might be one, too. I might have hidden Paul in my room, and he could force him to give up the telegram at the point of the revolver. Blackmail? A pair of criminals. Where is Dorsday? Dorsday, where are you? Can he have killed himself in remorse for my death? He'll be in the card-room. That's where he's sure to be. He'll be sitting at a card-table. If he is, I'll signal to him from the doorway with my eyes. He'll get up at once. 'Here I am, my dear young lady.' His voice will have that tone in it. 'Shall we go for a little walk, Herr von Dorsday?' 'If you like, Fräulein Else.' We cross the Marienweg to the woods. We are alone. I open my coat. The fifty thousand are owing. The air is cold, I get pneumonia and die ... Why are those two ladies looking at me? Do they notice anything? Why am I here? Am I mad? I'll go back to my room, dress quickly, put on the blue dress with the coat over it, but open, then no one can think I had nothing on before ... I can't go back. And I won't go back. Where's Paul? Where's Aunt Emma? Where's Cissy? Where are they all? No one will notice ... They can't notice. Who's that playing so nicely? Chopin? No, Schumann.

I flit about in the lounge, like a bat. Fifty thousand! Time passes. I must find that accursed Herr von Dorsday. No, I must go back to my room ... I'll drink some veronal. Only a few drops, then I shall sleep well. After work is done rest is pleasant ... But the work isn't done yet ... If the waiter takes the black coffee to the old gentleman over there, everything will go all right. And if he takes it to the young married couple in the corner, all is lost. What? What's that? He's taking the coffee to the old gentleman. Triumph! Everything will go all right. Ha, there are Cissy and Paul. They're walking up and down in front of the hotel. They're chatting quite gaily. He isn't particularly excited about my headache. Humbug! ... Cissy's figure isn't as good as mine. Of course, she's had a child ... What are they talking about? If only I could hear them! Why should their conversation interest me? I might go out, say good evening to them, and then flit on over the meadows, into the woods, climb up, clamber higher, higher, up to the top of the Cimone, lie down, go to sleep, and freeze to death. Mysterious suicide of young Viennese society lady. Dressed only in a black evening coat, the beautiful young lady was found dead in an inaccessible spot on the Cimone della Pala ... But perhaps they won't find me ... Or not till next year. Or even later. Decomposed. A skeleton. Better to stay in this warm lounge and not freeze to death. Well, Herr von Dorsday, where are

you hiding? Am I bound to wait? You must look for
me, not I for you. I'll look in the card-room. If he
isn't there, he has forfeited his right, and I'll write to
him. You were not to be found, Herr von Dorsday.
You relinquished your right of your own free will.
This does not release you from your obligation to
send the money at once ... The money. What
money? What's that to me? I don't care whether he
sends the money or not. I'm not the least bit sorry
for Father. I'm not sorry for anyone. Not even for
myself. My heart is dead. I believe it has stopped
beating. Perhaps I've drunk the veronal already.
Why does the Dutch family stare at me like that?
They can't notice anything. The porter's looking at
me suspiciously too. Has another telegram come?
Eighty thousand? A hundred thousand? Address still
Fiala. If there was a telegram he'd tell me. He looks
at me respectfully. He doesn't know that I've nothing on under the coat. Nobody knows. I'll go back to
my room. Back, back, back! If I tripped on the stairs
it would be a pretty sight! At the Wörthersee three
years ago there was a lady who bathed without a
costume. But she left the same afternoon. Mother
said she was an opera singer from Berlin.
Schumann? Yes, Carnival. He or she plays very well.
The card-room is on the right. Your last chance,
Herr von Dorsday. If he's there, I'll summon him

with my eyes and say to him: I'll be with you at midnight, you beast ... No, I won't call him a beast. But I will afterwards ... Somebody's following me. I won't turn round. No, no.

"Else!"

Oh Lord, Aunt Emma! Straight on!

"Else!"

I can't help it, I must turn round ...

"Oh, good evening, Aunt Emma."

"Oh, Else, what's the matter with you? I was just coming up to see you. Paul told me — oh, how dreadful you look!"

"How do I look, Aunt Emma? I'm feeling quite well again. I've just had some food." ... She's noticed something, she's noticed something!

"Else — you've — no stockings on!"

"What did you say, Aunt Emma? My goodness, I haven't any stockings on! No — !"

"Aren't you well, Else? Your eyes — you're feverish."

"Feverish? I don't think so. I've only had the most fearful headache I ever had in my life."

"You must go to bed at once, child; you're as white as a sheet."

"It's the light, Aunt Emma. Everybody looks white in this lounge."

She looks down at me so strangely. She can't notice anything? I must keep my self-control. Father is lost if I don't keep my self-control. I must say something . . .

"Do you know, Aunt Emma, what happened to me in Vienna one day this year? I went out in the street with one yellow shoe on and one black one . . ."

There's not a word of truth in that. I must keep talking. Only what shall I say?

"Do you know, Aunt Emma, I sometimes have fits of absent-mindedness like that. Mother used to have them too."

There's not a word of truth in that.

"I'll send for the doctor."

"But, Aunt Emma, there isn't one in the hotel. They'll have to send for one from somewhere else. He'd think it a fine joke, being sent for because I had no stockings on. Ha, ha!"

I oughtn't to laugh so loud. My aunt's face is distorted with fear. My behaviour seems uncanny to her. Her eyes are staring out of her head.

"Else, have you by any chance seen Paul?"

Ah, she wants help. I must control myself, things are critical . . . *"I think he's walking up and down in front of the hotel with Cissy Mohr, if I'm not mistaken."*

"In front of the hotel? I'll call them both in. We'll all have some tea, won't we?"

"I'd like to."

What a silly expression she puts on! I nod to her quite amiably and innocently. She's gone. Now I'll go

91

to my room. No, what shall I do in my room? It's high time, high time. Fifty thousand, fifty thousand. Why am I hurrying so? Slowly, slowly ... What do I want? What's the man's name? Herr von Dorsday. Funny name ... Here's the card-room. A green curtain in front of the door. One can't see anything. I'll stand on tiptoe. A rubber of whist. They play every evening. Two men are playing chess over there. Herr von Dorsday isn't here. Victory! Saved! But how? I must go on looking for him. I'm condemned to look for Herr von Dorsday till the end of my life. He's sure to be looking for me too. We always miss one another. Perhaps he's looking for me upstairs. We'll meet on the stairs. The Dutch people are looking at me again. The daughter is quite pretty. The old gentleman has spectacles, spectacles, spectacles ... Fifty thousand. It isn't so much. Fifty thousand, Herr von Dorsday. Schumann? Yes, Carnival ... I studied that myself once. She plays well. But why she? Perhaps it's a he. Perhaps it's a professional. I'll just look into the music-room.

There's the door. Dorsday! I'm on the point of fainting. Dorsday! He's standing by the window, listening. How can it be? I'm eating my heart out ... I'm going mad ... I'm dead ... and he's listening to a strange lady playing the piano. There are two men sitting on the sofa. The fair one only arrived today. I saw him get out of the carriage. The lady's no longer young. She's been here for a few days. I didn't know she played the piano so beautifully. She's

all right. Everyone's all right. It's only I who am damned. Dorsday! Dorsday! Is it really him? He doesn't see me. He looks like a respectable person now. He's listening. Fifty thousand! Now or never. Open the door softly. Here I am, Herr von Dorsday! He doesn't see me. I'll signal to him just once with my eyes, then I'll lift the coat a little, that'll be enough. After all, I'm a young girl. I'm a respectable young girl of good family. I'm not a prostitute ... I want to go away. I want to take veronal and sleep. You've made a mistake, Herr von Dorsday, I'm not a prostitute. Good-bye, good-bye! ... Ah, he's looking up. Here I am, Herr von Dorsday. What eyes he makes. His lips tremble. He fixes his eyes on my face. He doesn't suspect that I've nothing on under the coat. Let me go, let me go! His eyes are shining. His eyes are threatening. What do you want of me? You're a blackguard. Nobody sees me but him. They're listening. Come along then, Herr von

Dorsday! Don't you notice anything? There in the armchair ... good God, in the armchair ... why, it's the rascal! Heaven be praised! He's back, he's back! He'd only gone for a trip and he's here again. The Roman head is here again. My bridegroom, my beloved! But he doesn't see me. And he shan't see me. What do you want, Herr von Dorsday? You look at me as though I were your slave. Fifty thousand! Does our agreement still hold good, Herr von Dorsday? I'm ready. Here I am. I'm quite calm. I'm smiling. Do you understand my look? His eyes say to me: Come! His eyes say: I want to see you naked. Well, you swine, I am naked. What more do you want? Send the telegram off ... at once. Thrills run over my skin. The lady goes on playing ...

Delicious thrills run over my skin. How wonderful it is to be naked. The lady goes on playing, she doesn't know what's happening. Nobody knows. Nobody sees me yet. Rascal, rascal! Here I stand naked! Dorsday opens his eyes wide. At last he believes. The rascal gets up. His eyes are glowing. You understand me, beautiful youth!

"Ha, ha!"

The lady has stopped playing. Father is saved. Fifty thousand. Address still Fiala.

"Ha, ha, ha!"
Who's that laughing? Is it I myself?
"Ha, ha, ha!"
What are all these faces round me?
"Ha, ha, ha!"
How stupid of me to laugh. I won't laugh. I won't.
"Ha, ha!"
"Else!"
Who's calling 'Else'? That's Paul. He must be behind me. I feel a breath on my bare back. There's a humming in my ears. Perhaps I'm dead already. What do you want, Herr von Dorsday? Why are you so big, and why are you flinging yourself on me?

"Ha, ha, ha!"

What have I done? What have I done? What have I done? I'm falling. It's all over. Why has the music stopped? An arm is put round my neck. That's Paul. Where's the rascal? I'm lying here.

"Ha, ha, ha!"

The coat is thrown over me. And I'm lying here. The people think I've fainted. No, I haven't fainted. I'm perfectly conscious. I'm a hundred times awake, a thousand times awake. Only I can't help laughing.

"Ha, ha, ha!"

Now you have your wish, Herr von Dorsday. You must send the money for Father at once ...

"H a a a a a h!" ...

I don't want to shriek and I can't help shrieking. Why can't I help shrieking? ... My eyes are shut. No one can see me. Father is saved.

"Else!" ... That's my aunt ... *"Else! Else!"* ... *"A doctor, a doctor!"* ... *"Run for the porter!"* ... *"What's happened?"* ... *"Impossible!"* ... *"Poor child!"* ...

What are they talking about? What are they muttering? I'm not a poor child. I'm happy. The rascal has seen me naked. Oh, I'm so ashamed! What have I done? I'll never open my eyes again.

"Please shut the door."

Why shut the door? What a murmuring! A thousand people are crowding round me. They all think I've fainted. I haven't fainted. I'm only dreaming.

"Try to calm yourself, gnädige Frau." ... *"Has a doctor been sent for?"* ... *"It's a fainting fit."*

How far away they all are. They're talking from the Cimone.

"We can't leave her lying on the floor." ... *"Here's a rug."* ... *"A blanket."* ... *"A blanket or a rug – it doesn't matter."* ... *"Quiet, please."* ... *"On the sofa."* ... *"Will you please shut that door?"* ... *"Don't be so nervous, it is shut."* ... *"Else! Else!"*

If only my aunt would be quiet!

"Do you hear me, Else?"

"You can see that she's unconscious, Mother."

Yes, thank God, I'm unconscious for you and I'll stay unconscious for you.

"We must take her to her room."

"What's happened? Good Heavens?"

Cissy. How did Cissy come to the meadow? Ah, but it isn't the meadow.

"Else!" ... *"Please be quiet."* ... *"Please step back a little."*

Hands, hands under me. What are they going to do? How heavy I am. Paul's hands. Go away, go away. The rascal is near me; I can feel it. And Dorsday's gone. They must look for him. He mustn't kill himself till he's sent off the fifty thousand. Ladies and gentlemen, he owes me money. Arrest him!

97

"Have you any idea who the telegram was from, Paul?" ...
"Good evening, meine Herrschaften." ... *"Else, do you hear
me?"* ... *"Better leave her alone, Frau Cissy."* ... *"Oh,
Paul."* ... *"The manager says it may be hours before the doctor comes."* ... *"She looks as if she were asleep."*

I'm lying on the sofa. Paul is holding my hand.
He's feeling my pulse. Quite right, he's a doctor.

"There's no question of danger, Mother. An − attack." ...
"I won't stay in the hotel a day longer." ... *"Please, Mother!"*
... *"We leave in the morning."* ... *"Just up the servants'
staircase."* ... *"The stretcher will be here in a minute."*

Stretcher? Haven't I been on a stretcher once
before today? Oh yes, it was my bier that I was lying
on. I was dead, wasn't I? Must I die again?

*"Herr Direktor, couldn't you make the people get away from
the door?"*

"Don't get so agitated, Mother."

"It's so inconsiderate of people." ...

Why are they all whispering? As if they were all in
a death-chamber. The bier will be here in a minute.
Open the gate, champion.

"The passage is clear." ... *"People might at least have
enough consideration to − "* ... *"Please, Mother, don't get so
agitated."* ... *"Please, gnädige Frau."* ... *"Won't you look
after my mother for a few minutes, Frau Cissy?"* ...

She's his mistress, but she isn't as pretty as me.
What's that? What's happening now? They're bring-

ing in the stretcher. I can see it with my eyes shut.
That's the stretcher they use when accidents happen.
Dr. Zigmondi, who had that fall on the Cimone, lay
on it. And now I'm to lie on the stretcher. I've had a
fall too ...

"Ha!"

No, I won't shriek any more. They're whispering.
Who's bending over my face? There's a nice smell of
cigarettes. His hand is under my head. Hands under
my back, hands under my legs. Go away, go away,
don't touch me. Shame, shame! What do you want?
Leave me alone. It was only for Father's sake.

"Carefully, please, like that, slowly." ... "The rug?"
..."Yes, thank you, Frau Cissy."

Why is he thanking her? What has she done?
What's going to happen to me? Oh, how good, how
good! I'm floating, I'm floating. I'm floating in the
air. They're carrying me, carrying me, carrying me
to my grave.

"Oh, I'm used to it, Herr Doktor. We've had heavier people
than her on it. Once last autumn we had two at once." ...
"Ssh, ssh." ... "Would you mind going on, Frau Cissy, and
seeing that Else's room is ready?"

What business has Cissy in my room? The
veronal, the veronal! If only they don't pour it away.
Then I should have to jump out of the window.

99

"Thank you very much, please don't trouble any more."

"I'll inquire again later."

The stairs are creaking. The stretcher-bearers have heavy mountain boots on. Where are my patent leather shoes? They've been left in the music room. They'll be stolen. I wanted to leave them to Agatha. Fred gets my fountain pen. They're carrying me, they're carrying me. Funeral procession. Where's Dorsday, the murderer? He's gone.

The rascal has gone too. He's gone on his travels again. He only came back just to see my white body. And now he's gone away again. He's walking along a giddy path between a cliff and a precipice ... Goodbye, goodbye ... I'm floating, I'm floating. Let them go on carrying me up, further up, up to the roof, up to the sky. It would be so comfortable there.

"I've seen it coming on, Paul."

What has Aunt Emma seen coming?

"I've seen something of the kind coming on for several days past. She's quite abnormal. Of course she must go to an asylum."

"But, Mother, this isn't the time to talk about that."

Asylum? Asylum?

"You don't really suppose, Paul, that I'll travel to Vienna in the same carriage with her like this. One might have unpleasant experiences!"

"Nothing whatever will happen, Mother. I'll guarantee that you won't be caused the slightest unpleasantness."

"How can you guarantee that?"

No, Aunt Emma, you won't be caused any unpleasantness. Nobody will be caused any unpleasantness. Not even Herr von Dorsday. Where are we? We've stopped. We're on the second floor. I'll just open my eye for a second. Cissy's standing there in the doorway talking to Paul.

"Here, please. Yes, here. Thank you. Move the stretcher quite close to the bed."

They're lifting the stretcher. They're carrying me. It feels good. Now I'm home again. Ah!

"Thank you. That's right. Please shut the door ... Would you mind helping me, Cissy?"

"Oh, with pleasure, Herr Doktor."

"Slowly, please. Take hold of her here, please, Cissy. Here, close to her legs. Carefully. And then ... Else ... do you hear me, Else?

Why of course I hear you, Paul. I hear everything. But what does that matter to you? It's so nice to be unconscious. Oh, do as you please.

"Paul!"

"Yes, gnädige Frau?"

"Do you really think she's unconscious, Paul?"

'Du'? She calls him 'Du'! I've caught you! She calls him 'Du'!

"Yes, she's quite unconscious. It's usually so after attacks of this kind ..."

"Paul, It's enough to make one die of laughing when you put on your grown-up doctor airs."

I've caught you, you humbugs! I've caught you!

"Be quiet, Cissy."

"But why, if she can't hear anything?"

What's happened? I'm lying in bed with nothing on under the blanket. How did they manage that?

"Well, how is she? Better?"

That's Aunt Emma. What does she want now?

"She's still unconscious."

She's creeping round on tip-toe. She can go to the devil. I won't be taken to an asylum. I'm not mad.

"Can't she be brought back to consciousness?"

"She'll soon come to, Mother. She needs nothing now except rest. So do you, Mother. Won't you go to bed? There's absolutely no danger. Frau Cissy and I will look after Else during the night."

"Yes, gnädige Frau, I'll be chaperone, or Else will be, according to the way you look at it."

Wretched woman. I lie here unconscious, and she makes jokes.

"And I can rely on your waking me, Paul, as soon as the doctor comes?"

"But, Mother, he won't be here till tomorrow morning."

"She looks as if she were asleep. Her breathing is quite quiet."

"It is really a kind of sleep, Mother."

"I can't help still being upset, Paul. Such a scandal! You'll see, it'll be in the papers."

"Mother!"

"But she can't hear anything if she's unconscious. We're talking quite quietly."

"The senses of people in this condition are sometimes preternaturally acute."

"You have such a learned son, gnädige Frau!"

"Please go to bed, Mother."

"We go tomorrow morning, whatever happens. And we'll get a nurse for Else at Bozen."

What? A nurse? You'll find you're mistaken ...

"We'll talk about all that tomorrow. Goodnight, Mother."

"I'll have a cup of tea brought up to my room, and I'll look in here again in a quarter-of-an-hour."

"There's absolutely no need for you to do that, Mother."

No, there's no need. You can go to the devil. Where's the veronal? I must wait. They're going to the door with my aunt. No one can see me now. It must be on the table by the bed, that glass of veronal. If I drink the whole glass all will be over. I'll drink it in a minute. My aunt has gone. Paul and Cissy are still standing by the door. Ha, she kisses him. She

103

kisses him. And I'm lying with nothing on under the blanket. Aren't you ashamed of yourselves? She kisses him again. Aren't you ashamed of yourselves?

"Now I know she's unconscious, Paul. If she hadn't been she'd certainly have sprung at my throat."

Won't you do as I ask you, Cissy, and be quiet?"
"But why, Paul? Either she's really unconscious, and if so she can hear and see nothing, or else she's making fools of us, and it serves her quite right."

"Someone knocked, Cissy."

"I thought so too."

"I'll open the door quietly and see who it is ... Good evening, Herr von Dorsday."

"Excuse me, I only wanted to inquire how the patient is." ...

Dorsday! Dorsday! Does he really dare? All the beasts are let loose. Where is he? I hear them whispering outside the door. Paul and Dorsday. Cissy is standing in front of the mirror. What are you doing in front of the mirror? It's my mirror. Isn't my reflection still in it? What are they talking about outside the door, Paul and Dorsday? I feel Cissy's gaze. She's looking across at me from the mirror. What does she want? Why is she coming nearer? Help! Help! I scream and no one hears me. What do you want by my bed, Cissy? Why are you bending over me? Do you want to strangle me? I can't move.

"Else!"

What does she want?

"Else! Hear me, Else!"

I hear, but I say nothing. I'm unconscious. I can't talk.

"Else, you've given us a nice fright."

She talks to me as if I was awake. What does she want?

"Do you know what you did, Else? Just think, you went into the music-room with only your coat on, and suddenly you stood there undressed before everyone, and then you fell down in a faint. They say it was an hysterical attack. I don't believe a word of it. I don't believe you're unconscious either. I'll bet you can hear every word I say."

Yes, I hear, yes, yes, yes. But she doesn't hear my yes. Why not? I can't move my lips. That's why she can't hear me. I can't move. What's the matter with me? Am I dead? Am I pretending to be dead? Am I dreaming? Where's the veronal? I want to drink my veronal. But I can't stretch out my arm. Go away, Cissy. Why are you bending over me? Go away, go away. She'll never know that I heard her. No one will ever know. I shall never talk to anyone again. I shall never wake up again. She's going to the door. She's turning round once more to look at me. She's opening the door. Dorsday! He's standing there. I've seen him with my eyes closed. No, I really see him.

105

My eyes are open. The door is ajar. Cissy is outside too. Now they're all whispering. I'm alone. If I could only move now.

Ha, I can, I can. I move my hand, then my fingers, I stretch out my arm, I open my eyes wide. I see, I see. There my glass stands. Quick, before they come into the room again. Are there enough powders? I must never wake up again. I've done what I have to do in the world. Father is saved. I could never go among people again ... Paul is peeping through the doorway. He thinks I'm still unconscious. He doesn't see that I have my arm almost at full stretch. Now they're all three standing outside the room again, the murderers! ... They're all murderers, Dorsday and Cissy and Paul; Fred is a murderer too, and Mother is a murderess. They've all murdered me and pretend to know nothing about it. She killed herself, they'll say. You've killed me, all of you, all of you. Well, have I got it at last? Quick, quick! I must. I mustn't spill a drop. There. Quick. It tastes nice. More, more. It isn't poison at all. Nothing ever tasted so nice. If you only knew how nice death tastes! Goodnight, my glass. (Klirr, klirr.) What's that? The glass is lying on the floor. It's lying down there. Goodnight.

"Else! Else!"

What do they want?

"Else!"

Are you here again? Good morning. I lie unconscious with my eyes shut. You'll never see my eyes
again.

"She must have moved, Paul. How else could it have
fallen?"

"It might possibly have been an unconscious movement."

"If she isn't awake."

"What are you thinking of, Cissy? Just look at her."

I've taken veronal. I'm going to die. But everything is just as it was before. Perhaps it wasn't
enough .. Paul's taking my hand.

"Her pulse is quiet. Don't laugh, Cissy. Poor child!"

"I wonder if you'd call me a poor child if I'd gone and
stood in the music-room naked!"

"Be quiet, Cissy!"

"As you wish, sir. Perhaps you'd rather I went away and
left you alone with the naked Fräulein. But please don't be
shy. Just behave as though I weren't here." ...

I've taken veronal. Good. I'm going to die. Thank
God.

"By the way, it looks to me as if this Herr von Dorsday is
in love with the naked Fräulein. He was as upset as if the
matter concerned him personally."

Dorsday! Dorsday! Why, that's the – Fifty thousand!
Will he send it? Good God, if he doesn't send it! I
must tell them! They must make him do it. God, if all
this has been for nothing! But I can still be saved.

Paul! Cissy! Why don't you hear me? Don't you know that I'm dying? But I don't feel anything. I'm just tired. Paul! I'm tired. Don't you hear me? I'm tired, Paul. I can't open my mouth. I can't move my tongue, but I'm not dead yet. That's the veronal. Where are you? I shall go to sleep in a minute. Then it will be too late. I don't hear them talking at all. They're talking and I don't know it. Their voices buzz so. Oh, Paul, please help me! My tongue is so heavy.

"I think she'll wake up soon, Cissy. She looks as if she were trying to open her eyes. Oh Cissy, what are you doing?"

"I'm only putting my arms round you. Why shouldn't I? She wasn't shy either." ...

No, I wasn't shy. I stood there naked before everybody. If I could only speak you'd understand why. Paul! Paul! I want you to hear me. I've taken veronal, Paul, ten powders, a hundred. I didn't want to do it. I was mad. I don't want to die. You must save me, Paul! You're a doctor. Save me! ...

"She seems to have become quiet again. Her pulse — her pulse is fairly regular."

Save me, Paul! I implore you! Don't let me die! There's still time. But then I shall go to sleep and you won't know it. I don't want to die. Please save me. It was only for Father's sake. Dorsday insisted on my doing it. Paul! Paul!

"Look here a minute, Cissy, doesn't it seem to you that she's smiling?"

"Well, Paul, it's only natural she should smile, when you're holding her hand so tenderly all the time."

Cissy, Cissy, what did I ever do to you that you should be so cruel to me? Keep your Paul – but don't let me die. I'm so young. It will grieve Mother. I want to climb a lot more mountains. I want to dance. And I want to marry some day. I want to travel. Tomorrow we'll do the trip up the Cimone. Tomorrow will be a lovely day. The rascal will come too. I'll invite him humbly. Run after him Paul, he's going along such a dangerous path. He'll meet Father. Address still Fiala, don't forget. It's only fifty thousand, and everything will be all right. They're all marching in convict's clothes and singing. Open the gate, champion! It's all only a dream. And here comes Fred with the hoarse girl, and the piano's standing out in the open air. The piano-tuner lives in the Bartensteinstrasse, Mother! Why didn't you write to him, child? You forget everything. You ought to practise your scales more, Else. A girl of thirteen ought to be more hard-working. Rudi's been to the fancy-dress ball and didn't come home till eight this morning. What have you brought for me, Father? Thirty thousand dolls. I shall want a house of my own for them. But they can go for walks in the

garden. Or they can go to the fancy-dress ball with
Rudi. Hello Else. Oh, Bertha, are you back from
Naples again? Yes, from Sicily. Let me introduce my
husband, Else. Enchanté, Monsieur.

"Else, do you hear me, Else? It's I, Paul."

Ha, ha, Paul! Why are you sitting on the giraffe on
the merry-go-round? ...

"Else, Else!"

Don't ride away from me. You can't hear me if
you ride so fast through the Hauptallee. You must
save me. I've taken veronal. It's running over my
legs, right and left, like ants. There, catch him –
catch Herr von Dorsday! There he goes. Don't you
see him? He's jumping over the pond. He's killed
Father, run after him. I'll run too. They've strapped
the stretcher on to my back, but I'll run too. Where
are you, Paul? Fred, where are you? Mother, where
are you? Cissy? Why do you all let me run through
the desert alone? I'm frightened all alone. I'd rather
fly. I knew I could fly.

"Else!"

"Else!"

Where are you? I hear you, but I don't see you.

"Else!" ...

"Else!" ...

"Else!" ...

What's that? A whole chorus? And an organ too? I'm singing too. What song is it? They're all singing. The woods, too, and the mountains, and the stars. I've never heard anything so beautiful. I've never seen such a clear night. Give me your hand, Father. We'll fly together. The world is so beautiful when one can fly. Don't kiss my hand. I'm your child, Father.

"Else! Else!"

They're calling me from so far away. What do you all want? Don't wake me. I'm sleeping so well. Tomorrow morning. I'm dreaming and flying. I'm flying ... flying ... flying ... asleep and dreaming ... and flying ... don't wake me ... tomorrow morning ...

"El ..."

I'm flying ... I'm dreaming ... I'm asleep ... I'm drea ... drea – I'm ... fly ...